THE MUSE OF MISSING PIECES

THEA HAWTHORNE

Contents

A note from the author v

Chapter 1 1
Chapter 2 8
Chapter 3 15
Chapter 4 23
Chapter 5 32
Chapter 6 40
Chapter 7 51
Chapter 8 59
Chapter 9 65
Chapter 10 74
Chapter 11 81

An Extra Chapter 87
Afterword 95
Acknowledgments 97
About the Author 99
Also by Thea Hawthorne 101

A note from the author

The Muse of Missing Pieces is a cosy fantasy romance with low-stakes and low-angst. It contains one fade-to-black scene and some adult language.

This novella uses Australian/UK English spelling and conventions, which may differ slightly from those familiar to US readers.

If you'd like to find out more about the world of Esk and stories within it, follow my newsletter here:

www.theahawthorne.com/newsletter

THE OLD TOWN
THE REED BED
TO THE GARDENS
THE RIVER LUNE
HARRIET
STUDIO
GUILD HALL
ARTISAN'S QUARTER
WILLOW ISLE
ARTEMISIA
AN ILLUSTRATED SECTION
OF THE TOWN OF
ESK

Chapter One

Rainy days always bring miserable luck. And in Esk, where it rains more often than not, Harriet's bad luck never runs dry. The grey skies are so ever-present that when a rare clear sky comes along, everyone scurries away from it like field mice when a barn blanket is lifted. Rain is a comfort for most townsfolk, but not for Harriet.

She leans on the counter and watches as rain drips down the bookshop windows and turns the world outside into meltwater. Colette says people buy more books in grey weather, and Harriet isn't going to argue with the person who employs her. Gods know, she needs the wages. Her tiny pocket of an apartment has rent due, and she's scraping the bottom of her purse. The artisan's guild covered it last time she struggled, but now the guild's membership fees are due, too, and she can't cover those, let alone the debt she still owes them. She's near entirely out of what little luck she's survived on, this last year.

If she could just think of something to draw, she might push herself out of this rut, but her head is as empty as the pages of her sketchbook, and it's been a year and there's never a shred of an idea for her to seize. She tries, but her hands have lost the knack. She fears her muse is never coming back, and if it doesn't, it will be no one's fault but her own that she wasn't good enough to survive as an artisan.

There is no one who can help. She is the only one who can push past this horrid tangle she's in, but she doesn't know how. And until she figures it out, she's stuck behind the counter of Colette's bookshop, with barely enough hours each week to make a decent income. When she'd had commissions going, the scarce bookshop hours had been a blessing. Now, they're just not enough.

The Reed Bed is not the worst place to work, otherwise. If nothing else, she likes the company of books.

"Flood warning," says Colette, coming down the narrow staircase from the upstairs storage. "Saw the flags from the window."

She balances a parcel in her arms, wrapped in the brown paper and golden band of Belvine Press. It's blocking her sight, but Colette trots up and down those steps a dozen times a day and so makes it safely to the ground without struggle.

"Arrived last night," she says, dropping it on the counter with a satisfying *thud*. "There's fourteen more parcels upstairs."

Fourteen. There are few authors that Colette buys in such excess. Harriet tugs at the wrappings. "Starling's latest?"

Colette nods. "You'll take one and read it for me so we can sell it properly. I'll hardly have time."

She's being kind. She knows Harriet couldn't afford such a thing, not this week, and they're expensive books. Each paperback has a beautiful border of mountains and storms, and Harriet takes one with reverence. *When Winter Comes Swift.*

She's been a fan of Aster Starling since she'd picked up the first in the series, sitting behind the counter in this shop two years ago, still sore and prickly and full of shame. Starling's first book had been a bit prickly and sore, too, and had felt like a friend at a time she'd had none. She turns the book over in her hand, runs soft fingers down the spine. Maybe good things happen on rainy days, after all. "It's unlike you to leave a Starling unread for a moment. What's keeping you?"

Colette pulls a book out from her apron pocket. It has warm, tea-coloured covers soaked in gold and the silhouette of an airship in the centre. "The third *Golden Captain* book. It's not to be on the shelves for another week, mind."

"That's for the best. The shop will be overrun if they're out on the same day."

"Wouldn't it just." Colette taps the edge of the novel with a considering air. "You'll be alright down here? I might go upstairs, count the stock."

"Oh, go read your novel," says Harriet. "And I'll sit here and read mine."

Colette smiles and does so, disappearing into the quiet of the upstairs office. Perks of being the owner, Harriet supposes. She'll have to make do with perching behind the counter and reading between customers.

The tale pulls her in with alacrity. Aster Starling dives her right into a storm that is nothing like Esk's moderate rain clouds. No, he's on a mountainside and the storm is breaking over him.

...At such times, when my boots are full of water and the

slick cold of the rain drags itself down my back, I keep myself going forwards by filling my head with all the things I am running from. I won't detail such things here, but we all have them, do we not?

Starling has a way, she thinks, of speaking right to the heart of his readers. Of speaking to her.

She turns the pages, rapt. The rain thickens. The windows warp under the dance and wash of the water. A few soggy customers come through and Harriet watches their damp hands with sparrow-sharp eyes. She's relieved each time they leave, because she can get back to reading.

When she's disturbed for the sixth time, she doesn't bother hiding her scowl.

The roar of the rain slips inside with the customer. Water clings to her rush-gold hair in silver drops and the evening light cuts her silhouette against the dim windows. She looks around the shop and settles on Harriet.

"Harriet Finch?"

Harriet rests her finger against her page. "Yes? Can I be of help?"

"I certainly hope so." Behind her water-marked spectacles is a wide gaze that flicks from Harriet's head to her toes. Her warm brown eyes are the only clue Harriet has that the woman is anything other than marble, because everything else about her is as still and stiff as a statue. "Have you a few moments to spare?"

Harriet gestures to the empty shop. "Go ahead."

Not a speck of a smile touches the woman's lips as she approaches. "My name is Artemisia Whitaker. I'm a mosaicist, and I've a proposition for you."

Harriet stares. *Whitaker.* It's not an uncommon name—

the family is a sprawling one—but it's still a cursed thing to hear that name spoken in her presence. She swallows. "I'm not taking on any work. I'm done with that."

Whitaker's mouth twitches, like she's cut short a frown. She's maybe a palm taller than Harriet, with her hair pulled back in the sort of twist that is common amongst artisans. She's wearing a brooch of tesserae mosaic, though Harriet couldn't say what it is of, not without getting closer.

She's not inclined to get closer.

"It's for the Gardens," says Whitaker. She pushes the books on the counter aside—doesn't glance twice at the new Starling—and puts down a leather folder. "And before you say you don't believe me, you can see for yourself."

Gods be merciful, but Harriet looks. Any artist would, failure or not. A commission for the Gardens is the sort of thing that an artisan works a lifetime for. It is not something offered to a washed-out artist in a bookshop on a dingy spring evening.

"I've a chance to design a floor mosaic for the threshold between the Salon and the bathing gardens. They only accept a few commissions annually and this year is a competitive one. I am determined it will be my win."

Harriet flicks through the papers. There's the guild notice, with the mention of the commission, addressed to Whitaker. She must be well-respected, to have been approached personally with such a prestigious offer. Below that, the writ of work from the Gardens, along with a sketch of the space and dimensions. And below that, a piece of older paper, a bit battered at the edges and smudged with pencil.

Her mood is still somewhat curious and, not expecting

any daggers to the back, she unfolds it. The roaring in her ears swells, like the river itself has broken into the shop.

"Where did you get this?"

There's a fragile pause. "From my sister," says Whitaker. "Lucinta Whitaker."

Harriet folds the paper back up. Her fingers are numb, and the river swells inside her, bitter and dark. "Kindly leave," she says, and the words come out sharp. "I'm not interested."

Whitaker's brow drags down. It's a thorny look. "I want to use the design, Finch. It's an *excellent* design. I came here to ask you to work on adapting it to a mosaic. A collaboration. We can both share this commission—"

"No. Find another artist's work." Hot anger surges in her and she crushes the paper in her grip.

Whitaker grabs her wrist. The press of her skin is warm, shocking. "I don't want another's. I want yours."

"My name doesn't carry much weight these days. You'd best find someone else."

"Your design is the only one I've seen that comes close to being worthy of the Gardens, Finch."

The awful thing is, Harriet can see Whitaker means it. She might be the only person left in Esk that sees anything of worth in Harriet's work. She allows Whitaker to rescue the paper from her fingers.

"Sorry." For a moment she is truly, sincerely sorry. "But please leave. I don't want to see that design ever again."

Whitaker looks to the ceiling as if asking for the divine intervention of the ancient gods. "It's the *Gardens*. Didn't you ever dream of such a thing?"

"Don't appeal to my dreams. I don't have any left." If she ever has to see that mural sketch again, she might be sick with it. She'd thought it the best thing she'd ever done, once. She'd been *proud*. It had been a rude awakening, what had happened after.

She sets her jaw and stares Whitaker down. Whitaker huffs.

"Fine," she says. "If you insist on being stubborn, I won't waste any more of my evening." She pulls a mother-of-pearl case from her pocket and passes over a calling card. "My studio address. Come by if you find a lick of sense. I can wait until the end of the week, but after that, your chance is gone."

Chapter Two

Three long days pass, and the memory of that old sketch haunts her. She had thought it lost. Likely destroyed. Lucinta Whitaker, socialite and nightmare client, had destroyed the final work, after all. Why would she have kept the preliminary sketch?

She should send a note. Tell Artemisia Whitaker to use the design as it is or find a different one. But instead, she ignores the calling card tucked into her journal and continues with her week. And it's a cursed, unpleasant week.

The rain doesn't stop, for one. For another, it's the time of month that her brother insists on meeting her for tea, and so, despite her sour mood, she tucks herself into the corner of a crowded tea shop and waits.

It's a small shop, beside a channelled rivulet that directs meltwater through the streets of Esk. She perches against the window, her back to the room of chatting patrons. She's brought a journal out of habit, and she's moving her pen on the pages in a sad pantomime of drawing.

The lines tangle into a mess. She truly has lost the knack

of it, and she doesn't think it's ever coming back. In her grimmer moments, it feels as if Lucinta Whitaker destroying her mural had erased the work right back to the heart of her. *All* the work. The tempestuous joy of inspiration is now stagnant and blank. A blank heart, blank wall, blank page. It is all cold, vacant nothing.

Her pen moves, though. She blinks at her page, because it's no longer blank. She's started to sketch in a figure. Slight, straight-backed. Standing in a doorway cut out in storm-light.

Gods. She drags her pen through it, destroying it.

Artemisia Whitaker is not spending a crumb of time thinking about Harriet. Harriet shouldn't waste a scrap of thought on her, either.

Besides, she has other things to worry about. First amongst them: telling her brother that she has failed and that she's going to be kicked from the guild. He'll be disappointed in her. He's not the sort of person who ever fails at anything he sets his heart on.

The teashop door swings wide. A few early blossoms dance across the tiles, eddying around Rowan's feet as he strides inside. His cloak swirls, verdant as moss and trimmed in pale spring-leaf green. It's far too flashy for a teashop. He couldn't look more like a Gardens' nightingale if he tried.

"Harry," he says, spotting her and breaking out into a grin. He shrugs his cloak off and he's wearing silk. To a teashop. At midday.

She kicks out the seat beside her, dredges a smile from the writhing ocean inside her. "Did you make a choice to look like that today, or are you still dressed from last night?"

"You look like you forgot what a colour was a decade ago. Fabric does come dyed, you know."

He's changed the style of his beard, again. He is never quite the same each time she sees him. There's always something different, some new style he's trying. Perhaps it's a nightingale affectation, this shifting. Each time she sees him, he's a little more like a stranger.

He's still smiling, honest joy on his face. She hates that she's going to dint it with her news, but she has to tell him. She can't afford her dues and she'll never be able to settle her debts in order to pay. Even if she accepted Whitaker's daft offer, she hasn't the skills to meet it. Not anymore.

She shuts her journal. "I'll remember that the next time I have the coins to rub together."

"You'll have all the coins before too long, won't you?" He grabs her hands, squeezes her palms. "I'm so proud of you."

"Pardon?"

"The commission, Harry! I saw your name on the proposal for the new mosaic." He breaks away as the server comes along to deliver a tray of tea and biscuits. The teapot is green glass, the tea leaves swirling inside in mimicry of the weather outside as Rowan pours for both of them. "I'm so glad you decided not to give up. You are so talented. You only need a little faith in yourself."

Harriet accepts her tea with numb fingers. Her thoughts are spinning. Artemisia submitted her name on the commission proposal? The *gall* of her. The stinging, knife-edged *audacity*. She sips, the tea burning her lips. "I hadn't decided," she says, blank.

Rowan presses a biscuit into her other hand. "You can't back out now. I'm sure you'll win it. And I don't think anyone has twigged that you're my sister, yet, either. It'll be a grand reveal." He smiles, and it's the same dimple-cheeked smile he'd given her at six years old, when he'd been perennially sticky and forever talking about whatever nonsense had caught his attention.

She finds it hard to believe that he's made it to the upper echelons of the mysterious Gardens enclave. That he's one of the town's finest dance-masters and most desirable performers. That he's someone important.

He used to trip her into the river reeds and laugh. He used to drive her mad when he'd steal the best cushions and the best apples and the best spot on the sofa. He used to swap their midwinter gifts when he inevitably got a nicer one from their uncle.

Now he spends his days behind walls she can't cross through, and his winters rubbing shoulders with Esk's richest and finest. They say he's one of Madoc Casca's close confidants.

And he says he's proud of *her*.

She wants to break into crumbs, to be whisked away by the wrens outside the window, to be scattered so thoroughly no one will ever find her again. Instead, she takes a steadying sip of tea.

"That will be quite the reveal," she says, and manages a smile.

"You'll have to come see where the mosaic will go," he says. He digs through a pocket and pulls out a thin packet of finely made paper slips. They're printed in gold ink, the paper a deep green. There's four of them.

"Rowan," she says. "I don't need—"

"Just take them," he says, slipping them into her journal. "The bathing pools are good for you. I do worry you aren't taking care of your health."

"The remedial baths work just fine. It's the same water."

"But nothing compares with the Gardens," he says, earnest. "There's nothing more beautiful than bathing under the stars."

She thanks him, because what else can she do? These tokens will just join the others, unused, in her hall table drawer. She's never been able to muster the courage to bathe at the Gardens. It's far too much above her. It's far too revealing to be sitting in such undress amongst the fine and successful of Esk.

"Perhaps you'll find your muse again," he adds, and she knows he means it well. It still stings. "Have you any idea of the design yet?"

"Whitaker has some plans for me."

"Don't let her bully you. She's a fine mosaicist, but as far as I've heard, she isn't one for collaboration." He nibbles at a biscuit. "If you need any ideas, try brambles or river rushes or ivy. They're favourite motifs of Casca's. That will win you points."

She sighs. The tea spreads sweet and astringent across her tongue. "Don't get your hopes up, Ro. I haven't made anything in months."

"If it isn't working, just think of how it *might* work. You've always been too set in your ways. Be flexible."

"I think you're too flexible sometimes."

Rowan laughs. "I know you do."

They sit in silence for a while, watching the wrens flit through the young maple trees outside the window. A fine scattering of new leaves brightens the dark branches.

"What do you know of her?" Harriet asks, after her teacup is empty. "Whitaker."

Rowan shrugs. As a nightingale, he hears a great deal of gossip at society events. It's a part of his job, really, knowing who is who and what they've done. "She's popular, isn't she? Finest graduate of her year at the academy. She's known for making the little sweetheart tesserae that lovers are all gifting one another. I think her heart is in the more functional work, though. She's done a host of ornamentations for the stores on Gemina Street. Her speciality is thresholds, as I hear it."

"But what is she *like*?"

"How am I to know? I haven't met her. Haven't you met her?"

"In passing."

"Well?"

Harriet runs a finger down the edge of her journal, thinking. "She's forthright," she decides, though her mind also supplies *aloof* and *stiff*. "And oddly sincere."

Rowan blinks, then leans on the table between them. His blousy shirt drapes with his movement, all grace. "Those are very complimentary things to come from my famously picky sister."

"I'm not picky," Harriet says, bristling. "And they weren't compliments. Not exactly, anyway."

"To date, the nicest thing I've ever heard you say about anyone is when you said that bookshop owner of yours 'minds her own business'."

Harriet huffs, because he might be right. She pulls *When Winter Comes Swift* from her bag. "Here," she says. "Give it back, mind."

Rowan takes it, brightening up. "Oh, I forgot this was coming out. Please tell me he follows up on that curious happening with the night-chimes."

"In a fashion," she says. The book distracts him, which is what she intended. She quite unexpectedly has other business to attend to. "I've got somewhere to be. I'll see you next time."

"Stay away from the river. It's getting up," he says, before dragging her in to give her a kiss on the cheek. He is *such* a nightingale sometimes. She wishes she could move through life with the ease he does. Instead, everything always feels like such a fight.

Even this.

She doesn't want to do the commission. She doesn't want to work with Artemisia with her rain-dashed glasses and neat hair. But she doesn't want to disappoint Rowan, either. She can't let him down.

She steels herself at the street corner, then turns towards the artisan quarter. This is a commission that can save her, if she can pull it off. She only need make a few tweaks to a design she already has drawn. Barely a few days' work, if she can get her thoughts gathered together for long enough.

She does not check the calling card—she's been staring at it enough these past days to have memorised the address.

Willow Isle. Right in the middle of Esk. Right in the middle of the roaring River Lune.

Chapter Three

Willow Isle is soft with rain. The first spring blossoms hang waterlogged and ruined from glistening branches, and the stone paths reflect the aetherlight of the little teashops and studios in shimmering, golden images. The roar of the River Lune echoes through the streets, all around.

The address takes her to a narrow, tall building of honey-sandstone. The street-side door is the entrance to a tiny teashop, lit up golden in the gloom. An aetherlight sends a patch of light across the doorway and Harriet looks down to see a riot of splintered blues and greens beneath her boots.

A mosaic sits right through the doorway space. Tiled plum blossoms and autumn leaves garland the threshold and match the handsome blue tiles of the teashop inside. It's lovely work. It's strangely enchanting and graceful, the pattern of stone soft in a way that she didn't think stone could be.

Well, she's surely in the right place.

She leaves her bent-spoked umbrella leaning in the

doorway and steps inside. It's the usual teashop ambience, all curled steam and steeping tea leaves. Black-cloaked academics sit with their heads in their books like hunched ravens sheltering from the weather. A single gathering of artisans takes the bench by the rain-streaked windows.

None of them are Whitaker.

She steps up to the small counter and digs the calling card out of her satchel. "I'm looking for Artemisia Whitaker."

He squints at her. "She give you this?"

"Yes."

"Huh. She never allows visitors." He passes it back. "I suppose you can go up through there. Top landing."

He gestures to a gold-handled door at the back of the shop. The splendour of the teashop vanishes as soon as she's through. There's no aetherlight in the stairwell, just the dreary wash-water light from the tall windows. Even the steps are worn through and are in good need of a polish.

From the top landing, she can see right out over the Lune. The pale yellow flood flags are snapping in the wind, strung high across the footbridges and along the river path on the far side of the river. Across the landing, a short hallway stretches out towards four doors, each with a bronze nameplate. She knocks on the door titled *Whitaker*. An answering call comes, but it is far too muffled to understand. She knocks again.

"I said come in," comes the voice, closer, and then Whitaker yanks the door open. She stops. Looks Harriet over. "Oh. It's you."

Harriet sets her jaw and doesn't smile. "It is."

"Come to accept my offer?"

"I came to ask why my name is already on your proposal."

Whitaker scrunches her nose, shifting her glasses up. "Goodness. However did you find that out? Well, no matter. You really had better come in."

The studio is not nearly as dreary as she'd expected. The tall windows send smeared rain-shadows glancing along the length of the room, but Whitaker is clearly doing well enough to have installed two large hanging aetherlight pendants and their golden glow counters a great deal of the gloom. A half-done oil painting sits on an easel, pushed into the far corner, and there's a promising sculpture of a figure worked in clay tucked between a stack of books and a pot of tools.

A distinct smell of clay and dirt hangs in the air.

Whitaker claps her hands and a small cloud of dust billows up. "You *are* accepting my proposal, aren't you?"

Harriet turns back to her. Whitaker is watching, cool little mouth and lash-veiled eyes.

"I am." The words stick in her throat and hurt coming out. "Though I still think you've made a misstep by asking me, Whitaker."

"It's Artemisia," she says. She sits on a velvet-and-brass stool, propping her feet under the long trestle table that sits in the centre of the space. She pulls a wooden tray towards her with a rattling sort of sound. Inside, all the tiny pieces of tile and stone shift and slide towards her. "I liked it, you know. Your mural."

"The one your sister had painted over."

"She's a coward with no good taste." She picks out pieces of pale green, stacking them on the table beside her. "You never should have minded her."

Curiosity wins Harriet over, and she gets closer.

Artemisia is hunched over a design of leaping hounds and ancient forest. It's a traditional motif, the sort that is found in old friezes and tapestries.

"Who designed that?"

She tips her head to the side, considering Harriet. "How do you know it wasn't me?"

"If you could design like that, you wouldn't be chasing after my old work."

She huffs an almost-laugh. "This doesn't hold a candle to your work, Finch."

"It's Harriet," Harriet says, because she doesn't know how else to reply. "Why did you put my name on the proposal?"

Artemisia slides pieces of stone chips together, grouping them over the design. Emerald marble for rushes. Mint for the undergrowth. A murky river-green for the forest, cut through with copper crumbs. "I put it there before I approached you. It didn't occur to me that you would decline."

"Really?"

"The Gardens are about as prestigious as you can get, short of dealing with the Heirs or the House directly. I can't fathom why you wouldn't want to do it."

"I'd just about made my mind up to let my guild membership lapse."

The chips *tink tink* against each other in the silence. Finally, Artemisia sits back. "Well, that's foolish of you. I suppose I assumed you had more thoughts in that head of yours."

Harriet steps back, stung. Her lack of thought is exactly

the problem, and it's rude of Artemisia to prod at her so. "I haven't painted in near a year."

"Lazy and empty-headed," Artemisia mutters to the air. She stretches, goes back to her work. "Your design is for a full wall. I have a patch of floor the size of this table. You'll see the problem, I'm sure. I'm just asking you to rework the theme to flow just as gracefully in this space as it did in the old space."

"Just."

"Thirty percent of the commission value?"

Harriet blinks. "Forty," she says.

"*Forty*." Artemisia runs a hand down her face, clutches her chin as if in distress. "Fifty-fifty is the correct answer. You're meant to haggle."

"Why ask if you were going to give me fifty, anyway?"

"Because it's customary. Gods, anyone else would have let you short yourself on forty." She pulls another tray down, this one with pale yellow stone and ceramic tile.

Harriet isn't a fool. She just doesn't care enough to haggle, and besides, she's sure her contributions won't be worth fifty. "How much is the commission worth?"

The figure Artemisia returns to her makes her blink. Even half of that is more than she'd made in her best year of work as an artisan.

"I see why you want to win it."

"Do you?" Artemisia's fingers are fast with the chips of tile. Unerring, decisive. "It's not about the wealth of it, for me. Each sparkling face that turns out for Season this year will trip their way across that mosaic. They won't be able to ignore it."

She punctuates that with a *clack* of a tile. Whoever she is thinking of, it's clearly personal.

Harriet wanders along the length of the table, brushing her fingers across the trays. The chips of stone inside are jagged to the touch, bright and cold as river pebbles. "Why my mural?"

"As I said. I like it."

"You've clearly got access to artists far more accomplished than I."

"That's a matter of taste," Artemisia says. "And in this, my taste is all that matters."

"Would Lady Casca's taste not be the most important?"

"We will suit, no matter what we do."

Harriet wants to know what muses Artemisia has been praying to, to have confidence like that.

"Besides," adds Artemisia, "There's one more thing you might wish to know. The artisan I'm competing with is using a design by Nora Newell."

Another cursed name. Harriet picks up a piece of storm-grey marble. The edge is sharp. "You think I have a score to settle?"

"Do you?"

Does she? Harriet considers. Newell is the artisan that Whitaker contracted to destroy Harriet's mural. She wouldn't have taken it personally, only Newell had made a point of tracking Harriet down to make an amusement of her for it.

"I'll do what I can with the design," she says, picking up the folder Artemisia had been carrying when she'd come to the bookshop. "I'll borrow this."

Artemisia doesn't turn to see what she's picked up, just makes a noise of agreement.

"I'll have to work here," adds Harriet.

Artemisia's shoulders go stiff. "Whatever is wrong with your own studio?"

"I don't have one."

She makes a sound in her throat. Disappointment, again, with a dash of disgust. She lays down a tile with a clipped sound. "Fine. If that's what you need."

The window panes are darkening as the city sinks into night, the street lamps lighting up with a faint, amber glow.

"I'll be heading out, then," she says.

Artemisia looks up, tucks a lock of hair behind her ear. She frowns at the window, as if startled to see night has arrived. "The river is up," she says, after a moment. Her frown stays stubborn and faint between her brows. "Be careful."

Downstairs, the teashop is packing up for the night. The server nods to her.

"There's another door round the back of the stairwell," he says. "For future reference."

Harriet flushes, ducks her head in apology. Outside, her umbrella is gone. She sighs, pulls her coat collar higher, and sets off into the sheeting rain. The Lune heaves under the footbridge, high and restless, and the taste of river water is in the air, dampening her lips. It's a short, wet walk to her flat. She drips across her hall to the bathroom and leaves her clothes in a sodden heap in the bathtub.

It's raining harder, and Harriet doesn't want to get soaked again, so she has toasted currant buns for dinner as she sits by the fireplace and sets out the contents of the folder. The papers are damp at the edges, but mostly intact.

She'll have to change the entire shape of the composition to fit Artemisia's mosaic. It's a considerable amount of work, maybe even worth fifty percent of the ostentatious commission fee.

She should start on it. She'll need all the time she can get. Only it's cold and she's tired right through. Not the tired of weary limbs, but the sort of tired that sulks, heavy, in the heart of her and tears her vague thoughts of action into nothing.

Maybe tomorrow.

She sets another log on the fire and rolls into bed.

Chapter Four

In a fit of morning optimism, she catches a tram to the far side of the merchant district and pays too much for a roll of good paper and a handful of vine charcoal. Then, as the morning rolls on and the reality of her decision hits her, she slinks back to the artisan quarter and her tiny flat, hoping no one she knows sees her.

She hates the thought of someone spotting the supplies and knowing she's working again, as if the sting of failure will be less if no one knows about it. It's not true, though. It'll sting like paper cuts, regardless. And it's not like no one will know, anyway. Artemisia will know.

Artemisia, with her precise hands and her neat hair. With her studio scattered in paintings and sketches and sculptures, like she hasn't met a medium that doesn't melt into obedience under her touch. Like she has enough ideas that she can leave them strewn and unfinished, waiting for her attention.

Whilst studying at the academy, Harriet had spent years alongside people like that. Artists who effortlessly summoned delight into form, as if it was nothing special. For a while, she had fancied herself one of them. She'd learned better since.

The wide, blank roll of paper sits like a judgement in the corner of her faded parlour, and so she ignores it by unearthing her sketchbook. It's thin, half the pages torn out in a fit of frustration a year past, but she hasn't the money to be spending on a new one, and she hasn't the supplies to bind one herself.

She flicks through it once, puts it aside, and then it, too, sits like a judgement on her side table. She doesn't know what she's waiting for. A note from Artemisia? An invitation? By the end of the week, it's sorely obvious nothing is coming.

Finally, one morning, she unlatches her window for a breath of early chill, and decides she's dithered long enough. She brushes the damp plum blossoms from her windowsill, mind decided.

Lazy and empty-headed.

It's played over in her head for days, and she's been trying to figure out what Artemisia had meant by it. She had spoken it, cold and polish-smooth, like a passing thought, but not meaning to hurt.

When Newell had goaded Harriet on her failure, in the weeks after the mural debacle, those words had meant to hurt. Harriet knows what vitriol sounds like. Dislike, too. Artemisia's disdain was an aloof thing, restrained, and run through with an air of expectation, like how Rowan sounded when he was putting on airs to tease her.

The thought stops her short. Had Artemisia been *teasing*? Surely not. Artemisia Whitaker, finest graduate of the academy for her year, did not engage in friendly teasing with Harriet Finch, absolute no-one.

Her work at the bookshop takes her morning up in a hassle of book sales. The day is busy, and more than a few patrons stop to talk about the latest Starling. Before she leaves, Colette presses her into pasting up a set of large, printed posters announcing Flore's new release. The quality is good; it's proper printmaking from an artisan who knows their craft.

The figures are bold and strong, a golden airship captain and his brave crew. Her fingers twitch as she thinks of tracing her touch across them, learning the movement of those lines. There's something to learn from them, she thinks. An answer to one of her many problems.

Her attempts at restructuring her mural sketch have been coming along very poorly. Again and again, the lines have turned lifeless and dishonest beneath her fingers. Dust and lead, and very little life. Looking at these posters makes it clear just how inadequate her attempts have been.

There is no avoiding it. The muses have truly deserted her and it smarts, even though she'd been ready to abandon them first. She had not done a midwinter blessing. She had not sung in the dawning year. She had not drunk wine and recited poetry on the Night of the Muses. Instead, she had refused to make an offering and had spent the night alone, at home.

It is irritating how much she regrets that now.

At midday, she shoves her sketchbook into her bag and hurries towards Willow Isle. At the footbridge, she stops by a cart-seller to purchase a box of warm fruit tarts filled with fig and bramble jam. It's not the Night of the Muses, and Artemisia is no muse with an ancient altar, but she still feels braver knocking at Artemisia's door with an offering in her hands.

"Come back later," Artemisia calls from within, voice stretched cord-tight in irritation.

Harriet's bravery flees. "It's Harriet," she replies, or tries to. Her voice comes out as faint and faded as the wallpaper on the wall beside her. "Harriet Finch."

There's a space of silence. "Well, if it's *you*," Artemisia says, less sharp. "Come in."

Harriet edges into the room. The door shuts behind her.

Artemisia has her back to the door, a small chisel in one hand and a mallet in her other. Stone dust drifts in the grey light above her, like a smoke-made crown. "I was thinking you'd changed your mind."

The stove fire is lit, crackling loudly, and she places the tarts on the table beside it. "I'm here, aren't I?"

"You are. What did you bring?"

Harriet blinks, taken aback by the interest in Artemisia's face. It makes her look almost warm. "Fruit tarts."

Artemisia makes a hum under her breath and goes back to work, which appears to mostly consist of hitting larger slabs of stone with little care and sweeping the fractures into her colour-sorted trays.

"Having a bad day?"

"I'm having a productive day," she says.

"I do see that. Should I come back some other time?"

Another hit, with all the precision of a hunter's arrow. "No."

Artemisia *is* having a bad day. Harriet surely isn't being charitable with how that makes her feel a good sight better. Not even Artemisia is always loved by the muses, then. "I won't get in your way."

"Gods, please do," mutters Artemisia. Then she lays her

tools aside. "And I'll cease the hammering while you're here, I think. I do have some manners."

She points out the little desk she's cleared for Harriet, and then puts a kettle on the stove to heat. The desk, thoughtfully set up with a stack of paper, a tray of pencils and charcoals, and a sharpening-blade, knocks the cheer out of Harriet like a blow.

"So. Haven't painted in a year?" Artemisia perches on the edge of the desk, a fig tart crumbling between her fingers. "That's what you said, isn't it?"

"Not properly, no." She runs her hand down the cover of her sketchbook, but she certainly isn't opening it here, with Artemisia hovering over her. "Are you sure you want me with you on this?"

"Oh, no. Frightfully unsure," she says in a matter-of-fact way. "That's why I spent the effort of convincing you to join me. I do adore wasting my time."

Harriet stares. Artemisia takes a bite of her tart, and there's a twitch at the corner of her mouth.

Gods. She *is* teasing.

The kettle burbles in tuneless bird-song, and Artemisia slips away to tend to it. All the air runs out of Harriet in a rush. "That's good," she says, reaching for a pencil. They're much nicer than the cheap things in her satchel. Artemisia, clearly, buys herself quality. "Because I probably will waste it."

"Are you such a blanket all the time? Don't be a bore."

She's back in a moment to place a teacup at the edge of Harriet's desk. A gentle scent steams towards her, lightly floral and sweet. Artemisia pushes it in further, away from the edge, then balances one of the fig tarts on the edge of the saucer.

"They're nice," she says, and Harriet has the misfortune

of glancing up just as her mouth curls in what is, quite unavoidably, a smile. "You've good taste, Harriet."

They speak little, after that. The tea is strong, and the tarts are good, and the steady *clink* of Artemisia's work is soothing. It brings nothing new to Harriet's desiccated thoughts, though. After a few hours, she closes her sketchbook, trapping the smudged pages of half-starts inside, and bids Artemisia good evening.

She's back again the next day, because she might be a failure, but she's never been one to quit something before giving it an earnest try. They fall into a pattern. Harriet comes by on days she isn't working, and she brings offerings of food. Artemisia keeps their teacups topped up. They talk, sometimes, but mostly not.

Artemisia never asks her how it is coming along.

That last bit is the most important. Harriet had been tense as a storm for the first few days together, waiting for Artemisia to ask to see her work. But she never does. It's the only reason Harriet comes back, again and again. The only reason she keeps trying to dredge something useful out from her concepts and thoughts.

A week to the day she had first brought fig tarts, she's toeing open Artemisia's door with an apple cake in her hands. She doesn't bother knocking. The studio is starting to feel like her space, too.

Artemisia is, as always, at her trestle. "What is that?"

Harriet shuffles over to the woodstove. "An apple cake from the bakery by the map shop."

When Artemisia looks up, there's a red mark on her cheek from where her hand was propped. She smiles. "That's fancier than usual. Special occasion?"

"I felt like apple cake." There's no special occasion, only a growing sense of guilt that she has nothing to show for her days of work. Apple cake will not make her task any less overwhelming, or make her charcoal obey the command of her hands, though at least it brings out that half-smile on Artemisia's face.

Artemisia had said she was wonderful. Rowan had said he was proud. Harriet has had enough of disappointing people. If the inspiration won't come easily, she'll drag it out, piece by aching piece.

Perhaps the apple cake works, though, because as the day passes, a lopsided sort of *something* forms on her page. It's not good enough, not by far, but it's better than blankness. It's something to work with.

"Here," Artemisia says, placing a cup of tea on Harriet's desk.

Harriet closes her sketchpad before Artemisia can peek. "Thank you."

"It's sheeting down out there." Artemisia returns to her trestle, and Harriet follows, glad of a break. The drumming rain is as loud as a festival summons, shaking the windows. The aetherlamps on the street flicker in a sullen way, and the night is coming in early and fast.

"I shouldn't stay much longer."

"Finish your tea." Artemisia yawns, stretches her hands over her head. It makes her body a long line of tension, patterned with dancing rain-shadows. "It's not so late."

The tea is too hot to drink, but Harriet sips at it, anyway. "Are the fish coming along well?"

Artemisia snorts. "Nothing ever goes well until it's done. And even then, it's iffy."

The fish mosaic has been the bane of Artemisia's life for the past few days, or at least, that is what she claims. Harriet has been watching in fascination as it forms from dull stone to a shimmering fish-scale dance of pale creams and greys and lilac-blues.

On the trestle, wraith-like forms twist through a tempest, sharp-finned and dark-eyed. She sips her tea, considering. "Don't they look rather...well, *beast*-like?"

She's thinking of the beasts that spawn in the wild aether-storms that bloom out over the ocean. She's never seen such a storm—they don't happen as far inland as this—but she's seen the aethergraphs in the papers.

"Perhaps. I've been reading Starling's latest. It must have bled through." She sighs, wrinkling her nose. "This is why I don't do my own designs, if I can help it."

"Oh, but wasn't it glorious? The book, I mean. Not to say your design isn't also, because it is." She takes another gulp of tea. "But that *storm*. How do you think Starling ever survived it?"

"Good fortune or benevolent gods. He's lucky he was found when he was," decides Artemisia. A twitch of her mouth turns her smile into something a shade warmer than her usual. "Are you a fan?"

Harriet runs a finger along the pale body of a fish. It's reversed, currently, stuck onto a thin sheet of paper with flour paste. Artemisia will take it to install in its final location soon, no doubt. It's looking quite complete.

"I am. Are you?"

"I'm more a *Mystery of the Thorns* reader, myself," she says, naming one of Flore's earlier series.

Something about that is delightful. She likes the thought

of Artemisia curled in one of the generous window seats in warmer weather, reading the fantastical tales of an earlier age of history. "Then you have hidden depths."

"One can hope. It would be dreadful for an artist to be exactly what she seemed." Artemisia leans on the edge of the trestle. She tips her head, and it makes her face softer. The shadows flow across the curve of her brow, of her mouth. She reaches out and her thumb is warm when she drags it along Harriet's cheek.

"Charcoal," she says, holding up her hand to show the dark smudge along her skin. "You were working too intently."

Harriet was not. Harriet was barely working, merely staring at a mess of charcoal and thinking about apple cake and Artemisia, and not one of those thoughts made anything useful appear on her page.

"I really should go," she says, staring at the smudge on Artemisia's hand. The drumming rain thrums through her, kicking her heart up. She pushes her cup at Artemisia, who takes it with a frown. "Thank you for the tea."

"Safe travels," Artemisia calls after her.

She barely hears it, with how fast she flees.

Chapter Five

The bookshop is busy, so Harriet has a fair excuse for missing the next few days. Colette insists she read the latest *Golden Captain* too, and Harriet finds the time in amongst all the other tasks. It's not a hardship—Flore is one of Esk's favourite authors for a reason, and it's not only the mystery surrounding their true identity.

She wonders if Artemisia has read it yet, and what she might think of the story. She takes it home and reads until she's finished, and after, she dreams of airships and storms and golden kisses.

Halfway through the next morning, there is a knock at her door.

She answers it in her slippers, with toast crumbs at her mouth. She expects it to be Rowan, since he is the only person to know her address.

"Good morning. You aren't working today, are you?" Artemisia is pink-cheeked from the cold, bundled in a sleeveless sweater and russet-check trousers. She looks like she's going somewhere.

"How did you know my address?"

"Got it from the guild. That hill is a bit of a hike, isn't it?"

"I don't think so." She steps back, realising she's being rude. "Come in. I was only reading."

Artemisia heads straight to the parlour. It's easy to find, seeing as it is most of the flat. From the parlour, glass-paned doors open into the bedroom, and Harriet gently pushes past Artemisia to pull them shut. Artemisia has no need to see her tangled sheets and piles of clothes waiting for a trip to the laundry.

It's all sorts of strange, seeing Artemisia standing in her sparse parlour. She's all river-rush-brown and autumn gold amongst the drab greens and rose-pinks of Harriet's single armchair and faded rug. She's looking at the aethergraph on the side table, and tilts it towards Harriet in question.

"My brother." It had been Rowan's gift for her last birthday. He'd taken them to a picture studio, and she'd been stiff and dour through it all. Rowan is smiling for the lens, but Harriet appears just as uncomfortable as she'd felt. She wishes she had smiled for him. She wishes she looked as content as he does.

"He's a nightingale?"

"Yes. He's rather in the flock permanently now."

Artemisia raises her brows. "Well, that explains these, then." She pulls the bath tokens out of her satchel.

"How—"

"They must have slipped from your journal yesterday." She smiles, then, just a hint of one. "That's valuable currency to leave lying around."

"You can keep them," says Harriet, and leans past her to yank the side table drawer open. A scattered stack of identical bath tokens lies amongst assorted notebooks and charcoal boxes. "I've got enough of them."

"There's so many." Her voice is faint. "Do you *never* go?"

"The remedial baths, sure. I don't think all the fuss is worth it."

"But these are proper Garden tokens! I have to work for a certain height of client to get my hands on these, and even then, only when I'm fortunate." She taps the tokens against Harriet's chest. Harriet doesn't take them. "Fine. Let's go, then."

"What, now?"

"You said you had nothing on."

"I didn't, actually."

Artemisia shrugs. "You haven't said you *do*. Do you?"

Harriet does not, and she doesn't think of a lie in time, and that's how she ends up in the changing lounge at the Gardens, slipping into a bathing shift.

Great draughts of steam drift through the open windows, scented like rain and stone and thyme and fir. There's the distant sound of water trickling, and for once, it's not rain. It's the twisting, tangled streams that crisscross the mossy terraces of the Gardens, feeding the hot springs.

She turns and finds Artemisia already changed. They have both opted for the shifts the Gardens provide, simple, gathered affairs of fine linen and draping sleeves. It suits Artemisia very well, and for the first time in an age, Harriet's fingers itch for a paintbrush.

Artemisia has removed her glasses, and she's squinting slightly as she looks Harriet's way. "You'll have to lead me, I'm afraid. I'll tumble into a stream otherwise."

Harriet holds out her arm. Artemisia places her hand on

her forearm, so gently. Her fingers are warm, warmer than the steaming air, even warmer than the spring waters when they reach the edge of the bathing pool.

Harriet knows that's not true, not really, but she fancies she can feel the heat lingering against her, even when Artemisia moves away.

The main bathing pool is a handsome, tiled affair inside a half-open pavilion. There are a few scattered bathers, though the steam is generous enough that Harriet cannot recognise faces. Further along the next terrace, barely visible between the leaf bare birches and small, ancient oaks, a bathing party is alight with laughter as they relax in one of the natural pools.

But all in all, it's a quiet day. The hot water is bliss over her. It soaks her aches right away.

"My aunt was in the airguard," says Artemisia, settling in a submerged alcove beside Harriet. It allows them to sit with the water to their chests. "She always said she'd never recover from anything without the springs."

Harriet well believes it. The springs are the lifeblood of the Gardens, the lifeblood of *Esk*. They heal the scrapes and bruises and illnesses and maladies. They wash away the aether residue that clings to those that work alongside the Crown, or those that live and work in the airships that guard the isles. There is aether through all of Esk, soaked right through the bedrock. Everywhere, except in the Gardens.

It's a sacred place. A refuge. A place of healing and promises and revelry. Her brother is one of the important sorts that tend the waters and conduct the festivals and splendour-filled society revelries that mark the Season in Esk.

Harriet knows all this, but it's the first time in a long time that she has felt it. She takes a breath, filling her chest with that damp stone scent.

"Was?" she asks, softly.

"The storms, a few years back. The year the papers called the Summer of Sorrow. She was on the *Eder*."

Harriet swallows. The smothering warmth of the steam presses in. The airship *Eder* had been the head of the airfleet. When it had fallen, it had taken almost all its crew down with it. She remembers the papers. Esk had lost its admiral, an airship, and nearly lost its First Heir, too. The papers had talked of little else for weeks upon weeks.

"It was an awful time. I am sorry."

Artemisia's gaze is wide, a little blurry. Steam-damp curls of hair cling to her forehead and cheeks, and there's a pink flush across her cheeks.

"It was, wasn't it?" She sighs and folds back against the baths. "Everything really fell to utter ruin after that."

Harriet, who rather feels her life fell to ruin in the years after that, too, nods.

"Sit back," says Artemisia. "You look like you're half-ready to leap out of the baths, sitting so straight. You'll never have any good ideas, all tense and torn."

"Is that why we're here?"

"Mm. Do you think I haven't noticed you frowning at your sketchbook all day long? Clearly, you need to relax a little. Good art doesn't grow from strife."

Harriet laughs. She leans back gingerly. "I know some who would disagree."

"Well, I hardly care what *some* think. What do *you* think?"

She has her eyes closed, and so Harriet looks in a way she wouldn't, otherwise. Follows the curve of water across

Artemisia's cheek, to her damp hair curling beneath her ear, and down to the hazy cling of linen to her shoulders, draping over the curve of her breasts, drifting in the water around her elbows.

And then she looks back up, and Artemisia is watching her, a slight smile at her mouth. "Well?"

Harriet tips her head back to stare at the roof of the pavilion, face heating. The sunlight is sending water patterns dancing across the stonework. "I suppose I don't create anything from strife, so I must defend the truth as otherwise."

"Exactly," says Artemisia, content. "That's not to say that hardship cannot bring us the skills and knowledge to be more versatile, because it does. And I think versatility is the mark of a skilled artisan."

"Versatility? Truly?"

The water ripples as a bather leaves. The water-reflections shiver and scatter.

"What else? An artist who can realise their vision must be able to surmount their obstacles, and that adaptability marks their success. Even if that means working in a style or a manner different from their last work."

"I don't agree, though," Harriet says. She stretches out, unbending from her hunch, and her thigh brushes against Artemisia's bathing shift in the waters. "Versatility is well and good, but that's not why anyone falls in love with anything. We don't become captivated because it's *good* or *better* or *the best*. It's the glimpse of the artist that connects us. The viewer and the artist both being seen and seeing each other. Style can't be discounted, because that is the mark of the artist. Not something you've cultivated or practised, but something you *are*."

Artemisia half-turns to her, face alight with interest. "Then the artist can be seen in anything they do, regardless of mimicry or style. By your own argument, the artist cannot help but be seen when they create."

"Well, perhaps, but there's a layer of facades, isn't there? You aren't telling your own story if you've been getting distracted telling someone else's."

Artemisia hums, unconvinced. "How can the artist show their true self if they do not know it themselves, yet?"

"Why else are we creating art other than to find out?"

She is silent for a moment. "And I? I work with patterns and motifs that have been repeated for centuries. The small bit I add from my imagination is inconsequential in comparison. By your measure, where do I fall?"

"You transform each piece that passes beneath your hands." Harriet twists, so she's facing Artemisia. "Each stone you lay down is *your* decision, not someone else's, and so you are seen in everything you create. I'd wager anyone half-familiar with your work could pick your stones out from any number of your peers."

There is silence. The water nibbles at the bath's edge, and at Harriet's skin. She's flushed all over, inside and out, and she rather wants to sink into the water and dissolve entirely.

"*My*," says Artemisia, only it doesn't sound mocking. It's just an exhalation of a breath. "So there is some passion left inside you, after all."

Harriet blinks, hurt. "Did you think there was not?"

"I'd hoped," says Artemisia, and there's something so heavy in the way she says those words. And then the moment passes, and she smiles. "Are you still thinking of giving up your membership? Or will I have you stay in the ranks of us artists, still?"

Harriet sinks back into the waters. The blissful warmth rises to meet her chin. It's not that she is *thinking* of giving it up, it's that she may not have a choice. She doesn't want to smudge a perfect picture of a day with talk of debt and missed deadlines, and so she makes an indistinct noise, as if she hasn't decided yet.

"I'll convince you yet," says Artemisia, and lies back beside her.

Chapter Six

The day dawns fogged and miserable. Sleet greys up the windows and all of Esk is hunched inwards, as if desperate to keep its warmth protected. It's spring, but the mountains clearly don't agree—they've sent down the most biting of their winter weather.

Harriet turns her collar up and pulls a woollen hat down over her hair. The air tastes of fresh fallen snow when she steps outside. The honey sandstone of Esk is stained a dark tea brown in all the rain, the same colour as the madly racing Lune.

The streets choke with town carriages pulled by damp, restless ponies. None of them are going anywhere fast, but some people have the time to spend sitting in comfort. Some, like Harriet, weave amongst them on foot, going places faster but at the cost of cold-bitten noses and wet stockings.

Even the tram seems to trundle along reluctantly, stuffed like a baked fish, full of dour academics and stoic airguards on their way across the river to the university and docks.

The flood flags are deep yellow today. She hesitates at the

footbridge. The Lune leaps beneath, deafening in its hunger. The churning, dark waters have already swallowed the lower river path and the reed beds where the ducks usually bob. Wherever the ducks are now, it's nowhere near the river.

She steels herself and crosses the bridge at a fast clip. She'd told Artemisia she'd be by, and she means to keep her word.

The last day has had her thoughts in a tail-chasing circle dance of Artemisia's damp lashes against her flushed cheek, and the linen clinging to the curve of her back, and the way her fingers had rested, warm, on Harriet's wrist.

Despite the fierce cold of the spring storm, Harriet's cheeks are hot. She ducks her face deeper into her coat collar and forges ahead. It is only when she is at the teashop, and sees it is cold and dark and closed up, that she realises that perhaps she's been a fool. Artemisia may not have come in today. But then she sees the golden lights aglow in the top windows and knows she did.

When she gets upstairs, she goes in without knocking. Artemisia looks up from her table, blinking.

"Oh! The footbridge is still open, then?"

"Yes. Did you not cross it?"

"I live on the Isle," says Artemisia. She tips her head in a vague direction. "Down the other end."

Harriet's boots are damp, so she toes them off and leaves them by the stove. It's burning brightly enough that Artemisia must have been here for an hour or more already.

"I thought you might still have lived up the hill," she says, after a moment.

"With Lucinta? No." Artemisia puts aside the piece of stone she'd been cutting. "You look wet right through. Stand by the fire a bit. I'll put the tea on."

Harriet does as she is bid, shuffling aside when Artemisia brings the kettle out. She'd thought the studio a large space, when she'd first visited, but she is realising it is really not so. Perhaps the large windows deceived her. Perhaps she hadn't been so conscious, then, of the way Artemisia took up space, too.

"Here," says Artemisia, and brushes the damp hair from her face. "Let me tie it back. It'll drip all down your blouse like this."

She is caught between the hot iron of the wood stove and the hot press of Artemisia's fingers against her scalp and her neck. She takes a breath, and it is loud, even over the murmur of the kettle, even over the rage of the storm.

Artemisia doesn't appear to hear it. "Better."

Harriet brushes her hand to her nape and finds her hair neatly gathered in a ribbon. "I had better get to work. I had a thought in the night and I'm desperate to capture it."

"Don't stay too long." A frown creases down her brow. "The flood flags are up, and I'm sure we'll be cut off before nightfall."

"Is that common?"

"Once or twice a year, at the very least. We're all very prepared for it, here." She hesitates, and there's something on her lips, only she doesn't say it. The kettle pipes, then, clear and shrill, and she busies herself making the pot.

Harriet goes to her workstation. The rain is a constant hum in the background and it doesn't feel like a day for charcoal, dry and dusty as it is. She pulls out a pot of ink and an old, ragged brush, and that works better. Each bristle of her brush bends with her wrist and the lines fall where she wishes them to be. There is something good in what she is making.

Gods, she hasn't felt that in an age. In months. Years, maybe.

A sweetness kindles in her, an old euphoria brought to the surface. It's not the right design, not yet, but the shapes are right. The movement is right.

She can see the form of what she is striving after, at long last.

"Harriet," says Artemisia, as if she's been saying her name for a long time.

Harriet startles, the brush skidding along the paper. She shakes it out, frowning. "What is it?"

"Can't you hear it?"

She does, then. The low, rolling clamour of Esk's flood bell. It's the deepest and loudest of Esk's bells. She hasn't heard it in months. She curses, crosses to the window, dripping brush still in her hand. Outside, the footbridge has disappeared under the rolling swell of the Lune. The rain shatters against the window glass with such force that it's leaking in, gathering in a cold, dark puddle along the sill.

"Well." Artemisia casts a glance at the leaking window, and the churning ocean of clouds swallowing the rooftops outside. "I think you had best come home with me."

Harriet draws her breath in through her teeth, but when she glances at Artemisia, Artemisia is smiling, small and warm.

"If it's not too much trouble."

"It's no trouble at all."

Artemisia grasps her hand tight as they fight their way through the storm. Harriet has never held hands with a soul before, barring her brother or aunt when she was young. It isn't done, in Esk, to hold hands with another on the street.

And yet, Artemisia takes her hand and slides her fingers between Harriet's, notching them tight together in the way lovers might hold hands, in the soft privacy of a parlour or a town carriage.

Harriet notices very little of the storm.

It's almost too short, the battle down the twisting streets of Willow Isle. Before she wants it, Artemisia is drawing to a stop at a neat white door in a pretty line of townhouses. Or, they would be pretty if they weren't so drowned by the weather. The street isn't wide enough for a carriage, and so the press of buildings offers some shelter from the wind. At the very least, she can hear Artemisia talk again.

"It's small," she says as she ushers Harriet in.

Inside is a usual Esk townhouse, the sort that has a kitchen and a bathroom and a parlour downstairs, and the bedroom upstairs. Harriet hangs her dripping coat on the entryway hook and crouches to unlace her boots.

Artemisia hurries off, fussing with the fire in the parlour. By the time Harriet makes it in, she's already off again, and the stairs creak as she goes upstairs. Doing the same in the bedroom, Harriet assumes, and then feels an odd sort of way at that thought.

There's no sofa in the parlour. Instead, a pair of pretty armchairs pose beside a footstool. The second armchair is piled high with a stack of Academy periodicals. She could sleep passingly comfortably on the rug, she supposes. It's thick enough, and Artemisia surely has some blankets about.

She feeds the fire a small log. It's a large hearth for the space, the sort that can get properly roaring, and all around it is decorated with ivory tiles with raised roses. The mantel has a classical style, and is covered the length along with assorted knick-knacks. A brass heron, a vase of green glass, a bronze tray filled with rings and faux gems and glass pearls. A painting hangs over it, large enough that Harriet has to stand back to admire it properly.

And, well, Artemisia had been right. The room *is* small. Between the two armchairs and the footstool, there's barely room to squeeze past to the tiny writing desk in the nook beside the fireplace. A handsome stack of books runs along the top shelf, and above it, a series of sketches in simple frames hangs gallery-style against the wallpaper.

"Those were the works that got me into the guild," says Artemisia, coming back through with a tea tray.

"They're very...mournful." And they are. The designs are abstracted, but Harriet catches the form of people in flowing shifts, caught amongst green riverside tangles and scattered wildflowers.

"I was a mopey student, far too much sentiment." She unloads the tray. The teapot is absent, clearly still waiting for the water to boil. "I'm afraid I usually buy dinner from the food markets. We'll have to make do with apple buns."

It's not only apple buns. Artemisia lays out a soft, brined cheese, and olives, and some flatbreads that are a bit dry but crisp up nicely when they toast them on the hearth.

They eat as they flick through the latest periodicals. It really has been too long since Harriet last took any lasting glance at the artisan world, because all the goings-on are new to her.

"I don't know how you haven't heard of the Wisp Lane revival," says Artemisia, chewing on the edge of her bun. "It's all anyone talked about over the Season."

"All anyone talked about in *my* circles was that recent

novel by Valerin. I checked my windows were latched for a week after I read it."

Artemisia turns a page, thoughtful. She's in the armchair, reclining in a way that makes it very clear that despite her artisan life, she did, in fact, grow up in the high quarter. "Do you enjoy working in the bookshop?"

"I suppose. It certainly keeps me in books."

"But you don't miss making art?"

"I'm working there because I couldn't. I've barely painted a thing since—" She cuts off. Her fingers are holding the periodical tight, creasing the pages.

"Since my sister." Artemisia sighs. "I looked you up, you know, when I was trying to track you down. The guild didn't have a single record of a work or commission since Lucinta made such a hash of everything for you."

"It was difficult, for a bit," Harriet admits. "And then, after, once people started forgetting and began wanting work again, I couldn't. I just had nothing left in me. It's all been vacant and drifting. I thought it was gone for good."

"I'm sorry," says Artemisia. "You deserved better."

People have said *I'm sorry that happened* to her, before. They've said *these things happen,* and *that's part of being an artist.* Not one person has ever said she had deserved better treatment than she'd got.

Lucinta Whitaker had commissioned her to paint her conservatory with a scene of Eskan festivity. It was the sort of commission that would have vaulted Harriet's career up another tier, opened a circle of genteel and monied contacts that wanted halls and parlours and nurseries meticulously decorated, and so Harriet had launched herself at the opportunity with all she had. The design, she'd thought, was the best she'd ever done. Lucinta had loved it, for a short time.

And then the evening party, and Velina Masey, second child of the distinguished Masey name, had called it *trite* and *amateurish*. The next day, Lucinta had it painted over, entirely erased.

That, on its own, might have been possible to weather. But the papers had picked up on it, run a quaint society story on Lucinta Whitaker's poor choice of wall design, how *embarrassing* it was for her. Harriet was named as the artisan. Within a day, all her clients had withdrawn their commissions. She didn't attract a sniff of interest for over a year after. Such a small thing, and it destroyed her entirely.

Now, she sips her almost-cold tea, and shrugs. "I've moved past it."

Artemisia's gaze is sharp. It pierces into her, tugs at words and draws them out. "Have you?" she asks.

"I'm not ashamed of it anymore," she says, and the words taste true on her lips. She *isn't* ashamed of it anymore. "If anything, I'm angry."

"Good," says Artemisia, smiling ever so slightly. "Anger is something you can *do* things with."

"I wouldn't even have that if you hadn't come into the bookshop. I might never have picked up a pencil again."

"I don't believe that, and neither do you."

"Still, I owe you for it."

"You don't." She looks away, shifting. There's a sort of mulish discomfort to her. "I wasn't there selflessly." She sighs. "I *do* like your work, Harry. I promise I do. But I wanted that design for more than just its beauty."

Harriet is caught up on the *Harry*. No one calls her that

but Rowan. She doesn't even like it when Rowan does it, but she thinks Artemisia could call her that forever and it would never sound anything less than sweet.

"Luce is a prick," Artemisia says, then. "She kicked me out of our childhood house, and she's never once invited me to one of her society parties. She doesn't like having an artisan sister, though the gods know why, because it's entirely *respectable*. Personally, I think she's jealous because she's never had the backbone to stick with anything long enough to get good at it."

There's a petty sort of pinch to Artemisia's voice, and she remembers the way Artemisia had looked at the aethergraph of her and Rowan. In the entire parlour, there's not a single aethergraph of Artemisia's family or friends. "You wanted my mural because you knew she'd recognise it."

"Luce is a socialite, through and through. She never misses an Opening at the Gardens. She goes to the salons. She bathes with her friends. She will have to walk over our mosaic again and again. And each time she does, she'll have to recognise that it is *my* work. And what's more, she'll know *your* work, the work she deemed not worthy of her shitty conservatory walls, is worthy of the Gardens."

"Oh gods," says Harriet, in dawning delight. "Artemisia, you're spiteful."

Artemisia raises her brows a touch. "And if I am?"

"You might have said from the start that was the reasoning. I'd have joined with you more quickly."

"You don't mind?"

"Not a whit."

Artemisia laughs, then. "Gods, I thought you'd run a mile if you found out."

"Quite the opposite," promises Harriet. It's quite easy, then, to go to Artemisia and bend to kiss her cheek. It doesn't even take a thought. "Thank you for championing me."

Artemisia blinks up at her, brown eyes wide. "I just said I had all the wrong motives."

"I think you said you had all the right ones."

Artemisia reaches out and pulls her down, right into her lap. The air slips from Harriet's throat, and then Artemisia's lips are on hers, dry and warm and soft as the finest charcoal.

It has been a long time since she's kissed anyone and the thought has her pausing, suddenly far too conscious of what she is doing. Artemisia draws back in a heartbeat, a faint flush on her cheeks.

"No, wait," says Harriet, and takes her lovely face between her hands and brings their mouths together again. She tastes of honey and apple, and when Harriet kisses her deeply, she makes a sound low in her throat.

"I've been wanting to kiss you," she says, pressing the words against Harriet's mouth. "You were so pretty in the baths."

"Liar," says Harriet, and she can barely help her smile. "You couldn't see a thing without your glasses."

Artemisia laughs. "I could see more than I let on," she admits. "I would have been fine without you guiding me."

"Spiteful *and* deceitful. All the warnings about you were true."

"I'm afraid so," she says, and kisses her a third time.

Artemisia's fingers are as clever and unerring on Harriet's body as they are on the mosaics, never missing a piece of her. Harriet shivers as Artemisia traces her breast through her chemise, slips her hand to her hip and skates the soft skin there. She slides her hands up Harriet's thighs, gathering the soft linen as she goes.

Her fingers are clever and unerring and entirely sure in their craft. Harriet hides her face in the soft hollow of Artemisia's neck and thinks that *this,* perhaps, is the missing piece to everything. She'd been drifting along alone when she needn't have been. Needn't ever be again, perhaps, if Artemisia would have her.

"May I?" Artemisia pauses with her fingertips on Harriet's inner thigh. "Do you like being had so?"

"I'd like it very much. I think highly of your fingers."

"My fingers are good," agrees Artemisia. She kisses gently at her ear and whispers, "but my mouth is better."

And the thought of *that* is enough to melt her like candle wax.

"Arte," she says, barely countenancing the shortening because her tongue does it without a thought, "let me take you upstairs."

"Gladly." Her voice is as soft and hungry as the river under the storm. She eases Harriet's shift back down across her thighs with a lingering touch. "Come along, then. Take me to bed."

Chapter Seven

The grey quiet of early morning is heavy. Under the stillness, under the steady drip of the window eaves and the ticking of the mantel clock, is the breathless rush of a river in flood.

Artemisia is beside her, a long curve of deep slumber, her hair sweeping across the pillow. Harriet slips from under the covers and borrows the robe hanging on the wardrobe door. It's a warm, woollen thing, and she ties it firmly about her waist as she pads to the window.

Artemisia's narrow house peers out over a walking path, a stone wall, and sliver of tree line, and the river. Or, that is how it normally goes, Harriet supposes. Now there is only a river.

There is no way the footbridge will be open, nor the main bridge, either. And few would be brave enough to risk a boat when the river looks like that. There won't be any ferries from downstream, either, not for a good couple of days.

She won't be leaving the isle until the evening, at the earliest. It doesn't bother her as much as she thought it might.

She rouses the hearth and goes downstairs to set the

kitchen stove and the parlour hearth. While she's there, she finds her satchel and rescues her journal and pencils.

Back in bed, the picture forms under her fingers with all the speed of the Lune. The lines flow together, gather and swell. River rushes and tangled ribbons and brambles, because she was listening when Rowan had told her what the Casca heir liked.

A joyful, overgrown riverbank, she thinks. Life, tumbling down into dark waters.

Artemisia wakes sometime into the process, but she doesn't disturb her. It's only when Harriet finally sets her pencil aside that she takes the sketchbook.

"It's perfect," she says. "It's the right decision to change the border."

"I rather stole the idea from you."

"Oh. My river sketches?"

"If we create the border in this way, we can have the main dancing figure from my original mural as the centrepiece."

"It suits the Gardens well." Artemisia sets the journal aside, kisses her cheek. "The river is still high, by the looks of it. You had better stay tonight as well."

"You don't mind, do you?"

She smiles. "Not at all."

Once they're fed, bathed, and dressed, they check the house for leaks and damage, and then take the short walk to the studio to do the same. The window leak has left a small lake of rainwater on the tile floor, but Artemisia throws down a canvas cloth and says she'll fix it later.

That night, they toast the last of the apple buns on the hearth and eat them with strong, spiced tea, before Artemisia takes her hand and tugs her up to bed.

When morning comes, the river has subsided. Harriet's clothes have been beside the hearth, and she dresses with pleasure, settling into the warmth of them.

Artemisia watches her from the dressing table. She's still combing tangles out of her hair. It's soft and silken, but it tangles worse than a bramble patch in autumn. Harriet loves that she knows that, now.

"Come by the studio the day after tomorrow," Artemisia says. "We'll scale up the design so I can start on the stones."

"Not tomorrow?"

"I have to be at the Guild Hall tomorrow," she says, looking displeased. "They're pressuring me to formally establish myself as an atelier, seeing as I'm no longer working under anyone else."

"And you don't wish to?"

"I don't know." She shakes her head, as if banishing an unpleasant thought. "It's complicated."

An offer from the guild to endorse a new atelier is no small thing. It speaks to how well-respected Artemisia is, for them to be considering it. Harriet can't imagine why she wouldn't want it.

"Well, I wish you luck with it." She shifts, glances out the window. "I really should be going. Colette will wonder where I was yesterday."

Artemisia tips her head back for a kiss, and the press of her soft mouth is a soothing touch. "Safe travels home."

Downstairs, the house is lit with small, affordable aether-lamps affixed to the walls, each shaped like a bronze shell, but it's not so much light as to be radiant. She leans against the hall table to put her boots on—still slightly damp—and that's when she notices the stack of letters sitting on top. She's curious, so she sifts through them.

Commission requests via the guild, all of them. She counts ten, then stops. Some are open, others are not. That's a considerable number of requests to work through. She'd forgotten, for a while, just how far Artemisia had risen in the ranks of guild artisans.

She places the commission requests back in a neat pile. She remembers having such things before the mural disaster. She remembers how quickly they had disappeared after, too. Nothing in the artisan world is assured. Harriet may yet rise as far as she had fallen. Artemisia may yet fall from the heights to which she has risen. It only takes one misstep.

The river is gentling, settling back to a whip-fast, silent rush. It is skimming just beneath the damp footbridge when she reaches it. A set of grey-coated airguard are clearing flood-spill, hauling branches and tangled masses of rushes from the railings.

"It's sound," the closer one calls. "But careful crossing. It's as slippery as an eel's back. You wouldn't want to put a foot wrong."

It's good advice, she thinks, but she learned long ago how far a misstep can throw you.

Harriet is more nervous than she should be, going to Artemisia's studio with her master sketch done. Her thoughts are wispy and ragged-edged the whole walk over, making it entirely impossible to settle on anything. The finished work is rolled up and tucked under her arm, and she has the odd thought, as she is crossing the footbridge, of tossing it in the river and running home and never thinking about this terrifying thing ever again.

She's not even sure if she means the commission, or if she means the soft curve of Artemisia's lips. Either way, she is on edge and anxious by the time she jogs up the stairs to the studio.

Artemisia looks up, as she always does. Her hair brushes against her cheek as she moves, a graceful tumble that makes Harriet ache for her pencils.

"Morning," she says, and that one word makes all the thorny anxiety melt away.

"Morning. How did your meeting with the guild go?" She places her roll of paper desk, as if it is nothing of note at all. "Did they convince you?"

"Not yet." Artemisia props her head on her hand. The other hand rests on her work, shifting idly at this tile or that. "Come here."

Harriet does, and Artemisia tips her face up. After a moment, Harriet stoops to place a soft kiss at the corner of her mouth.

"That's a coy sort of kiss," Artemisia says. "Cooled on me, have you?"

Harriet's cheeks burn.

"Gods, you've come over shy." Her lips twitch into a delightful smile. She stands. "Did something happen?"

"I didn't want to presume," she says, bluffing through the traitorous skip in her chest.

Artemisia is the one who catches her face this time, holds her there through a sweet, silken kiss. "Presume away. I'd like you to presume, with me." Her breath skates against Harriet's cheek.

It doesn't help the blooming blush. "I'll be sure to remember it."

"Do." Artemisia sits back down, seeming pleased with herself.

Harriet has never thought smugness could look good on a person. Artemisia lives to make her change her mind, it seems. "Don't divert. Why are you still refusing to open an atelier? It's the clear next step."

She considers a sky-grey chip of marble, then switches it for one in tempestuous blue. "I don't like working with other people."

"You're working with me right now."

"You're different." She places the stone. Nudges it into position with her fingertip. "I mean that. You really are something different."

"And everything about you is something different, too."

"Good. I'd hate to be boring." Another clink of stone. "If I open an atelier, I'd have to take on assistants in time. An apprentice, eventually. I don't work with others. I'm not any good at it."

"I'd disagree."

Artemisia levels her with a severe look. "That this has worked at all, Harry, is entirely down to how pleasant and obliging you are, and how much time I have spent thinking about kissing you and wondering if you'd be as obliging underneath me. That's hardly a model for future colleagues, is it?"

Harriet fumbles her sketchbook. The papers scatter across

the floorboards like plum blossoms in a stiff breeze. "That's entirely unfair to say out loud."

"Is it? My apologies." She's back to smug again.

Harriet gathers up her papers. She's jumpy again, because she's going to have to show Artemisia her final work, and she's almost convinced herself that Artemisia will hate it.

She sets her sketchbook aside and unrolls the design. The edges hang off the desk and she pins it down with an empty cup. The charcoal has smudged a little in the rolling of it, but the design is clear.

A warm hand settles on her back. Artemisia looks over her shoulder.

"Oh," she says, soft. "You've done it."

Harriet brushes a smudge of charcoal back into place. She *has* done it. Somehow, her lost muse has found its way back to her like a storm-soaked cat slinking home after having had the household mourning. "I guess I had something left in me, after all."

"There was no question of that. No artisan is done before they even get started."

"Do you think you can work with it?"

Artemisia gathers up the ends of the paper roll, straightening it out as much as can with her arm span. The design is drawn to scale, and it isn't exactly small. The paper roll had taken up nearly the entirety of Harriet's parlour floor.

"I'm sure I can do wonders with it," she decides. "It's excellent work. I like how your mind thinks. It twists things together so wonderfully. Newell won't have a whit of a chance compared to this."

"I leave it in your capable hands."

"No," says Artemisia, then winces. "I mean, I'm sure they *are* capable, but you needn't leave. Stay."

It had only been a figure of speech. It hadn't occurred to Harriet to leave, in truth, so she nods and helps Artemisia clear a space on her trestle to lay the design out. Artemisia asks her opinion on this shade or that, and Harriet makes tea while she lets Artemisia talk herself through her decisions.

She doesn't feel at all in the way. And when Artemisia looks at the clock, and then at her, and asks if she wishes to get supper together before heading home, she feels nothing less than perfectly in place.

Chapter Eight

"So, how is it going?" Rowan leans on the table, head cradled in his palm.

They're in the same teashop as last time, a shared plate of cake on the table between them. It's a quiet day. An academic sits in the corner, reading through a heavy book. She's entirely in her own world and doesn't notice them, not even with Rowan's bright colours.

"Fine," Harriet says. "We've sorted out the design. Artemisia will submit it for consideration, I suppose. My part is over."

"So you won't be at the Gardens later this week?" He looks disappointed. "I thought you might both be there."

"For what?" She spears a piece of cake.

"Lady Casca is meeting with the artisans to hear their proposals. Not just the mosaic, but all the current projects going on," Rowan says. "It would make sense for you to be there, wouldn't it?"

It would. Only Harriet hadn't even known it was happening. She takes her time with her mouthful, sorting through the odd knot of emotions that suddenly snarls in her chest. "Artemisia is the lead artisan. She doesn't need me there."

"She's exactly as the rumours say, then. A loner." Rowan huffs and takes his own piece of cake. "Maybe I'll poke my head in, make sure she's giving you proper credit."

"*Rowan.*"

"What? It's a fair concern. She doesn't collaborate often, you know. I looked up her work at the guild hall—"

"What in the silver storm were you doing at the guild hall?"

"I was checking up. I didn't want anything unfortunate happening, not after *last* time. It's that awful woman's sister, Harry. Of course I was going to check up."

"Gods, Ro. Don't be a sap."

Rowan grins, wide and pleased. "Anyway, she never puts her name with anyone else's. So I'll go and make sure you get a look in."

"Don't. It's fine."

Rowan has that opaque expression he sports when he's planning to do exactly the opposite of what she has requested. She sighs.

"She's risking enough by working with me, with my reputation. There's hardly anything for me to lose. The one with a chance of getting tarnished is her. It's better that my name stays out of it." She pushes crumbs around the plate. "Or maybe not. Maybe if my name is on it, then if Lady Casca hates it, the blame will be on me, and Artemisia's career won't suffer for it."

"Don't be a mouse," says Rowan, thorny. "Don't get cowed by her just because she's got more patrons in her grasp."

"I'm not cowed. It's not like that."

"Then why are you looking so sorry for yourself?"

"Because I want this to be successful. I want Artemisia to have this victory." She gives her brother a hapless shrug. "I like her."

He blinks. His mouth falls open, just a touch. "*Harry.*"

"She's lovely. You'd like her too, I think."

"Not like you, I'd wager."

She looks down but doesn't refute him.

He grins, as if she's given him wonderful news. "It's about time you had a lover again. Though it's not the smartest, is it, falling into bed with an artisan you're working alongside? Seems like the sort of thing that ends up in the gossip column when it all falls apart."

"Thank you, Rowan. That's very helpful of you."

"I'm just saying—"

"I know what you're saying, you weasel. Look. Forget I said anything." She points her fork at him. "And leave all of this commission business alone. It'll fall where it will."

Despite saying all that, Harriet can't help but wonder. She has a shift at the bookshop that afternoon, and she sits through it, restless. Did Artemisia forget to tell her about the gathering at the Gardens? Or had she never meant to tell her at all? She half expects Artemisia to come through the bookshop door, river-rush hair gathered at the nape of her neck and that cool smile on her mouth, to tell her how her day has gone.

Plenty of people come through the door, enough to keep her on her feet most of the day, but none of them are Artemisia. Flore's new book is selling so fast that their fourteen boxes have been whittled down to two. She rereads

Colette's copy behind the counter in stolen snatches. It's no less romantic the second time around, all stormbeasts and noble, upright men, but every time she reads *golden* she thinks of someone else.

Colette shoos her out when the day fades and she steps out into the inky spill of Esk's nighttime shadows. Water clings to the air even though the rain stopped a day ago. The stone is damp and the roofs are dark and even here, higher on the hill, the ceaseless rustle of the Lune's hungry rush weaves under the rattle of the tram and the echo of pony hooves.

It all fades to a soft murmur when Artemisia steps into the laneway, acorn-brown coat buttoned right to her chin. She smiles.

"You weren't at home. I thought I might catch you here."

"I'm caught," says Harriet, shrugging her arms out in a hapless sort of gesture. Artemisia takes it as an invitation to hook her arm through Harriet's.

"I thought we might get dinner at the food market," she says. "We can eat at yours."

They settle into a warm sort of silence as they walk down the row of food stalls that run along the border of the artisan and old quarters. Artemisia doesn't like almonds, and Harriet doesn't like rabbit, but they settle on parcels of baked river fish with rosemary and lemon, and honey-rich sesame cakes for dessert, and they carry their winnings down the rickety stairs to the dark street where Harriet lives.

They sit on the rug in Harriet's parlour, and Harriet watches Artemisia lick the oil from the corner of her mouth, and feels dizzy. She's hungry, and she's tired, and she hasn't had a sensible thought in days, and mostly, she just wants Artemisia.

"My brother told me that you'll be at the Gardens later this week."

Artemisia glances up. The firelight catches at her eyes, makes them glow. "Yes. I'll find out for sure whether our proposal has been selected."

Harriet breaks off a corner of her cake and crumbles it between her fingers. "May I come with you?"

"If you'd like," she says, and a frown shadows onto her brow. "I didn't say anything because I didn't think you'd want to go. I'm sorry."

"The thought terrifies me," she admits. "But I mean to see this through."

Artemisia's smile is bright. "Then you'll do fine."

"I don't know how you sound so sure of me."

"I never bother being unsure of anything," she says, and there's a touch of honesty in it. "If I have to be unsure of it, it's not worth my time."

"You are very headstrong," decides Harriet, grinning. "Not a whit of caution about you."

"I'd rather say I was discerning, which could, in fact, be an abundance of caution."

"Lucky me, that your discernment is in my favour."

Artemisia laughs. There's a flush on her cheeks. It might be the hearth warmth. It might not. "I know I've made the right choice. And it *was* a bit of a choice. I had two commissions to choose from in a narrow time-frame, you know. I could only do one. I chose this one."

"What was the other?"

Artemisia looks a bit riversick. "The Guild Hall entrance."

Harriet stares. Stares some more. "*Arte.*"

"So you see, it will be mortifying if I don't win the Gardens one," she says, mustering an admirable flippancy.

Mortifying, she says. More than that, Harriet thinks. Devastating. Disastrous. If she cannot win the Gardens work, having turned down the guild, she'll become a joke. Harriet knows too well what that does to an artisan's client list. That stack of commission enquiries by Artemisia's door would vanish in a heartbeat.

"However did you get commission enquiries from both the Garden and the guild at the same time?"

She sighs, pushes her glasses straight. "Somewhere, the gods are laughing at me."

She's nervous about it. Harriet hadn't even thought it possible for Artemisia to feel nerves, but it's undeniable. Artemisia Whitaker has gambled her career and somehow, *somehow*, the gamble she took was *Harriet*.

"You should have said," she says, faint.

"It would have made you feel pressured. I didn't want you pressured." She tips her head. "Well, not too much."

"We'll get it," says Harriet, as if she can make it so just by saying it with enough conviction. If only it were that easy. If only she had an ounce of Artemisia's faith. "Tell me when and where the gathering is, and I'll be there."

Artemisia holds out a piece of honey cake, and Harriet eats it from her fingers.

It's all the sweeter for it.

Chapter Nine

On the day of the Garden's gathering, Harriet wakes with stone in her chest. She washes and dresses, combs her hair and cleans her nails. The stone dread slinks after her through the minutes, pressing closer in the spaces between her fussing.

She's about run out of things to do when a knock shakes through the flat. It's not Artemisia. It's a post runner, and he hands over a thin envelope and is gone before she's even cracked it open.

It's from the guild.

To the attention of Harriet Finch, it reads. *Please present yourself at the guildhall at your earliest convenience.*

She glances at the clock. There's most of the day ahead of her, and no excuse to avoid the summons. Of course, she regrets her diligence as soon as she's at the guildhall and being ushered into a tiny room.

Or perhaps it's not so tiny. Perhaps it is only that Guildmaster Callowan fills up so much space with her presence, her disappointment, and her stern-edged gaze.

"Harriet Finch," she says, and then lets the silence say the rest.

Harriet shifts. Straightens her back. "If this is about my membership fees—"

"It is. It is also about the debt outstanding, and about the complete lack of productive work from you in the last year. The Guild requires at least three official commissions or equivalent accepted work to retain your membership, Finch. We have been lenient, but we cannot accommodate you forever. You promised you would have work to submit to us by the new year. You did not."

Harriet presses her lips together. What can she say?

"We really have no choice but to end your membership." To Callowan's credit, she doesn't take any pleasure in it. "In a year's time, you'll be free to resubmit, though you'll have to present a qualifying work once more."

"I—" She swallows, but her throat has seized. Her chest shudders with each heartbeat and there's a rising tide inside her, one she knows too well. Hot and shame-flushed, bitter and loathing. "I'm working on something."

"Yes, I know. Whitaker has taken you under her wing." Callowan rests her chin in her hand. "It's not enough."

"Must you do this now? If I am not certified by the guild, I can't work for the Gardens," she says. The words scrape out from her, raw. "I can't be credited for my work."

Callowan's mouth pinches. "I'm sorry, Finch. Try again in a year."

"It's Whitaker's work that will suffer for this, too. Is that fair?"

"And? Whitaker has turned her shoulder to us repeatedly these last months. Perhaps this lesson is a necessary one."

The bitter tide wells up in her. She bites down on the words she wants to say, because they'd help no one, and Artemisia least of all. Instead, she tugs the brass pin from her collar and drops it on Callowan's desk. It glints, tumbles end over end, and Harriet is gone before it falls to a stop.

Her feet take her halfway to Willow Isle before she wrenches herself around. The thought of having to tell Artemisia this news scours her through. She'll write a note and explain why she cannot accompany Artemisia to the Gardens, after all. She'll tell Artemisia to do what she has to do to save their project.

She's twisted all through, and she doesn't know where to go. After a few turn-arounds, she ends up in a teashop and the server wordlessly brings her a tray of strong, sweet tea. She drinks her way through it, watching the rain track down the windows. Her mind is stunningly empty.

Try again in a year.

It shouldn't hurt the way it does. She had been planning to end the membership herself, just a handful of weeks ago. But that had been before Artemisia and steam-shrouded baths and swollen rivers. Before the charcoal had danced under her fingers once more. Before she'd remembered what it was to create something from nothing but a whisper of the muse.

She regrets it already, the way she'd so easily given in. She might have fought harder. Bargained, even. Callowan might have been persuaded.

Nothing for it now. It's another failure for Harriet Finch to swallow.

Good thing she's had practice.

It's late by the time she arrives back home. She doesn't

send a note. Instead, she flops in her armchair and stares at the cold hearth. The flat smells of damp and dust, and a little like the candles Artemisia lights in her studio. She tips her head, following the scent, and her cheek presses against a soft shirt hanging over the back of the armchair.

It must be Artemisia's, because she owns nothing so fine. It's soaked right through with the scent of fig and honey, and a warmth curls right through her. Had Arte gone home wearing one of Harriet's blouses instead?

It's foolish that such a thought makes her smile, even through her misery. Or perhaps it's not foolish at all.

She breathes, fills all the hollow spaces in her with that scent. It's late, but not entirely too late. If she gets ready fast, she may still arrive at the Gardens on time. She won't be winning any commissions for herself, but she can help win one for Artemisia.

And that, she realises, would feel almost as good.

✻

She is too late. The doors to the Garden Hall are closed. They're great solid things, shut fast, and she knows there isn't any point in trying to force her way through. The sinking disappointment burns her throat, drops right through her.

It's raining, because of *course* it is. She pulls her coat collar up and heads to the shadowed corner of the entrance alcove, where she knows there is a smaller door for less grand entrances.

She knocks. When there is no answer, she knocks again, harder.

The door swings in, silent, and a man peers through the gap. Harriet might say he had a charming face, only he's looking at her like she's brought a dead bird to his doorstep.

"Pardon," he says, the words dripping with disdain. "The doors have closed."

"Please, I'm one of the—"

"No late entry," he says, clipped. "The Gardens have a strict—" He breaks off, narrowing his eyes. His gaze flicks from her head to her toes, then settles back on her face. His scowl deepens. "What was your name?"

"Finch," she says. "Harriet Finch."

He purses his mouth. "Wait a moment, Finch."

The door slams in her face. After a few cold minutes, it opens again, and her brother is peeking out at her. "Harry?" He quickly tugs her in. "You know better than to be late!"

"I wasn't going to come," she admits. "I dallied."

Rowan pushes her through the entrance hall so fast she barely glimpses the magnificent mural there, all lit by golden lanterns of candlelight. He pulls her into a discreet doorway, hiding them away in a passage that is far humbler than the room they have exited.

"I'll smuggle you in, but you'll have to be quiet about it." He gives her a censorious sort of glance. "Well, that won't be hard. Honestly, Harry. Might you wear a *bit* of colour?"

"Rowan," she says, batting his hands away. "Be still for a moment. I need to tell you something."

He gives her that suffering look he perfected years ago. "Yes?"

"I had my guild membership revoked. I'm sorry. I should have told you sooner, but—"

He huffs. "Why are you worrying about that now? You've got a party to sneak into."

She looks him over. He isn't in evening wear. Not by nightingale standards, anyhow. "Why aren't you at the party?"

"Expressly forbidden," he says, cheerily. "Apparently, I'm too prone to altercations."

"Ro—" She starts, then gives up. He won't tell her anything, not now.

"First things first, always. And first is getting you where you should have already been." He's leading her along a network of smaller passages. This must be the nightingale's view of the Gardens, she supposes. The hidden layer behind the paint and ornamentation that society sees. "It's rubbish about the guild, and I know you must feel horrid, but it'll turn out."

Either Rowan hasn't a clue of how tightly the guild controls who is allowed to work to commission or sell wares, or he is too used to the life of a nightingale, living in the strange world of the Gardens.

"Here," he says, drawing them to a stop by a hidden door in a panel. He slips off one of his necklaces, a pretty thing of green and amber glass beads. He tucks it over her head. "A bit of colour. Now, this door will take you to a hidden entrance, so just slide from behind the tapestry and look like you've been there all along."

He takes her coat, and Harriet gives him a dubious farewell, but it's all rather simple in the end. The tapestry is a huge, heavy thing, but it is simple to step out from behind it and into the tumble and music of the evening party.

Everything is warm in candlelight. Under the stone-scent

of the springs and the riot of perfume is the melt of candle wax, the charm of flowering thyme and rain-wet moss. Harriet clings to the wall, trying to find Artemisia's rush-gold hair through the swirling crowd.

Harriet has never been to an evening party, let alone one at the Gardens. It's an informal one, a matter of business rather than society, but Harriet would hardly notice it with the way people have dressed. Half of Esk's notable artisans are in attendance, gathered around card tables or draped over low sofas. Harriet pays them little attention.

She's more taken by the art. There is so much *art*.

Paintings hang on the richly printed wallpaper, and statuettes bend and dance on plinths in shadowed alcoves, and each piece of furniture is a minor masterpiece in its own right. A chandelier of a hundred or more steady, bright candles hangs above them, sending down a rain shower of broken light.

"Harriet." Artemisia seizes her arm. She's beautiful, drenched in pale linen with a woven belt of beaded glass. The beads match the ones on her spectacle chain. "I thought you hadn't made it."

"I didn't. My brother had to smuggle me in."

"And thank the muses he did. I believe I'm putting my words entirely wrong in every conversation I have."

Harriet laughs, remembering the way Artemisia had asked for her help in the bookshop weeks ago. Arrogant, cool, and entirely untouchable. "I certainly won't make things worse, I suppose."

Artemisia brushes a hand down her collar, teasing at the embroidery. "You've forgotten your pin."

"I haven't." She catches Artemisia's hand, holds it there.

"I handed it into the guild today. Or rather, they demanded it back. It's my own fault, really. I dragged my heels too far, for too long."

Artemisia glances up. Behind the shine of her glasses, her eyes are very wide and very bright. "You don't mean—"

"I'm afraid you'll have to claim the work all as your own, if the Gardens is to pay you for it." She smiles, honest, even though she's sure some of her own bone-sharp disappointment tints it. "It's either that or ditch the project entirely, and I've decided I won't allow that."

A flicker runs over Artemisia's face, slipping her into something cold as marble. "That's not right," she says, low. "We did this work together."

"It's complicated. I owe some money to the guild, and I haven't done the work I promised—"

"*Harry*," Artemisia says, stricken. "Why didn't you tell me? I might have helped."

Harriet shrugs, unhappy. "I rather thought it might all turn alright, in the end."

"And so it will." She tugs at her own collar, a moment from snapping her own pin free. "We can walk away from this. There will be more commissions. We'll get more chances."

"No. No, don't do that. This is *your* commission. Don't sink it just because I missed a deadline too many before you ever met me."

"I couldn't have done it without you."

"That's nonsense. You could have. You would have. You've done a hundred wonderful things without me. You turned down the guild hall commission for this."

"Good," she says, vicious. "I don't want a guild commission, anyway."

"You are ridiculous," says Harriet, so fond and so full that all the stinging shame of it is washed clean away. She unhooks the pin from Artemisia's lovely fingers. "Come on, let's smile and make nice, and get you your commission. I won't settle for anything less."

Chapter Ten

In amongst the press of bodies and conversation, a nightingale is presiding over a table layered in crystal glasses of shimmering drinks. Artemisia takes two—one for each of them.

"Careful," she says. "I hear it's strong."

The liquor is as sweet as morning air on Harriet's lips, but she heeds Artemisia's warning and takes small sips. The party isn't quite as she had expected. There are no announcements or bestowments. Instead, Lady Casca mingles with the gathering, talking to this person and that. A small contingent of nightingales flock behind her, dressed in silks and glass beads and gold strands. They each seem almost as important as Lady Casca herself, greeting artisans and socialites alike.

Music weaves amongst the conversation and all the sculptures flicker, lifelike, in the candlelight. And yet, Harriet hasn't much chance to enjoy it. Artemisia had not exaggerated her troubles in charming potential patrons. She forges through every conversation stone-faced, chin tip-tilted in arrogance. It's not winning her any points with the society types who are here to find new artisans to adore.

Harriet gets to work. This, at least, is something she can do to help make things right. When it comes down to it, she and Rowan aren't *that* different. She smiles, just the right amount to make a conversation partner rise to the challenge of making her smile more widely. She turns every conversation back to the adoration of Artemisia's work. She charms them, because if they're charmed with her, they'll think themselves charmed with Arte, too.

Artemisia blinks at her askance as they move on from another conversation. Her brown eyes are alight with a calculating air. "However did you get so good at this?"

"I'm not sure. A survival skill, I suppose."

"One you might have thought to employ in your own defence at least once," she mutters. "Oh gods. There's Newell. Quick, let us look too busy to engage."

It's too late, of course. Newell is cutting right towards them.

"Whitaker. You made it." Newell glances Harriet over. "And Finch, if I recall rightly? Curious partnership."

"I look forward to seeing your design attempts," says Artemisia. "You never fail to surprise me, after all."

"Yes, it must be startling to see inspired work, mustn't it? You *do* struggle with it."

Artemisia looks bored. "Yes, yes. May we skip past all the pleasantries, Newell? I've other faces I'd rather be staring at."

Newell's mouth goes as small and pinched as an almond. Harriet has no idea of why that has struck so deeply, only it clearly has.

"You are on a downward slide, Whitaker," she hisses. "A year from now, no-one will remember your name, or your work."

"And who do you propose is rising to eclipse me? Not yourself, surely. You haven't managed it yet."

"You shouldn't covet victory quite so soon," says Newell. "I heard your partner is quite the dead weight lately. And society does look down on an artisan mired in debt. It doesn't speak of a reliable character, does it?"

Harriet goes winter-still. "Pardon?"

Newell's smile is small and thin. "Your debts, Finch. It's hardly a secret, is it?" She's talking a touch too loudly. The people surrounding them take notice, angle their heads to better eavesdrop.

The cold dread is back, pressing against her back like a lover about to bite.

"Be careful, Whitaker. That's all I'm saying. Finch rather has a reputation for sinking like a stone, doesn't she? And it's a bit hard to paint over a mosaic, when all is said and done."

Artemisia steps forward, lip curling up in a sneer that turns her face into something wicked. "If you want to get personal, Newell—" she begins, but Harriet never learns what getting personal might bring, because that is when the nightingales descend upon them.

The flock, that had, until then, been winging after Lady Casca, surrounds them entirely. A woman gathers Harriet around the waist, tugging her into her side, and a man has Artemisia, and another woman is leaning on Harriet's shoulder like a cat arching up against a favourite person. She leans in too close, and she smells like mint.

"Now, now," she says, lightly. Her hair drifts around her

in a pale cloud. "We've strict instructions to not let the artisans get their claws out."

Newell's face goes stiff. "We're all friends here," she says. "There's no quarrel."

The woman raises her brows. "Didn't look so friendly to me," she says, dismissing Newell with a glance. She leans into Harriet. "Lady Casca is so *very* interested in talking to you," she adds, then waves a hand at Artemisia. "And her, too."

The nightingales bundle them away with a graceful strength that brooks no refusal. The pale-haired woman takes Harriet's face in her hands and angles it into the candlelight. Her smile is bright and sweet as honey. "Yes, I see the resemblance," she says. "You have your brother's charm and his tendency for trouble."

"*Is* he in trouble?" Harriet asks, alarmed. *Altercations*, he'd said.

The nightingales all laugh, as if at some joke. Her captor must see her alarm because she pats her cheek. "Artisans are not the only creatures who can't resist poking a rival."

They're all still laughing when they deliver Artemisia and Harriet into the presence of Lady Casca herself.

Her eyes are deep summer-green, startling in their intensity, and her skin is the gentle gold of tannin waters, and her hair is as dark as thickets of brambles tumbling down a riverbank. Harriet thinks painters must pray to all the muses for a chance to have her under their brush.

"I've looked over the proposals," she says, after introductions. "I find myself quite taken with yours over all."

There's a gentle silence. She waits politely. Harriet looks at Artemisia.

Artemisia sets her jaw. "You are very gracious," she says, and stops.

Lady Casca arches a graceful brow. "Am I? I would think *you* gracious, if you would accept the commission."

Artemisia wets her lips, and Harriet can see the shape of a refusal on her lips.

"Of course we accept," says Harriet, smoothly talking over whatever Artemisia had been on the edge of saying. "Artemisia accepts."

Lady Casca smiles. It's all grace, but Harriet gets the distinct air that she is laughing. "Good. I look forward to seeing your work amongst my collection. It has such a delicate touch to it. I've heard admirable things about you, Artisan Whitaker. And this is your first collaboration, is it not?"

Artemisia's mouth does a funny thing. She grips her glass tight. "Unofficially, yes. And I think it will be one of my finest works to date."

"Unofficially?"

"I'm no longer a member of the guild, madam," says Harriet, sparing Artemisia the awkwardness. She tips her chin and meets Lady Casca's gaze. "So my part in the work will remain unknown."

"Ah. But your proposal promised a joint work between two celebrated artisans."

"The work remains unchanged. It should speak for itself, regardless of the names attached."

Lady Casca laughs. It's a beautiful laugh. "You are Rowan's sister, yes? I see you share the same nature. Well, no matter. Your name will be attached to the work, Artisan Finch. If your hands have touched it, then it is yours, too."

She has no idea what nature Lady Casca is referring to. She hopes it is a flattering one.

"But the guild—"

"These are the Gardens," she says, soft and entirely implacable. "No one dictates to a Casca in the Gardens, not even the guild. I wish for a piece from both of you. I will get it."

Artemisia grips Harriet's arm tight. "Thank you," she says. "We'll do good work for you."

"I know. That is why I chose you."

They both duck their heads in a bow, and then Lady Casca moves on to sweep up the next artisan she has chosen for the year.

Artemisia is still gripping her arm, her fingers digging into the soft part below her wrist. Harriet untangles her gently, and then slips their hands together. Hidden by their skirts, it's barely noticeable.

"There," she says. "We got your commission."

"We've got *our* commission."

Harriet nods, faint. "I'm going to tread on the guild's toes if Lady Casca follows through with that."

"Then tread away," decides Artemisia. "They can whine all they want."

And they will whine, she knows. It's hard to care right now. From across the room, the pale-haired nightingale tips her head in Harriet's direction and winks. Harriet hides behind her cup.

At the end of the night, there is a toast to all the successful artisans. Amongst the flushed cheeks and bright eyes, Harriet spies a fair handful of sour faces, too. Not every artisan has been successful in gaining a Gardens commission or a new society patron. Newell glares at them from across the room, and Harriet knows *that* quarrel is far from settled.

She toasts high and drinks deep, and if the wine is stronger than any she has had before, it hardly matters, because Artemisia's arm around her waist is warm and strong and keeps her close.

Chapter Eleven

They lay the mosaic in the first days of summer. The bathing pavilion is a gentled thing by day, windows flung wide and the breeze skittering across the marble floors and through empty rooms. There are no nightingales or passers-through in this section. It's been closed off until Artemisia is finished with her work.

Artemisia has completed most of the piece in the studio in quiet, focused concentration. Each section has been taken on paper backings to the Gardens, and pressed into mortar and left to dry.

They're blessed with pleasant weather, mostly. The rain comes on the last day of the installation, but by then the mortar is dry and beyond harm from the damp air. It's a gentle rain, coming in with mist that rolls down from the mountains and turns the world grey.

Harriet barely minds the weather, though. Not when the last of the paper is scrubbed away and Artemisia reveals the work, face-up and shining, for the first time.

There will be an official unveiling, later, in candlelight,

with people gathering in to admire and fuss and adore. But for now, it's just the two of them, standing back to survey the work.

The figures from Harriet's original mural are here, recognisable and graceful in their dance. Twisted garlands weave between their outstretched arms and into the brambles and rushes of the border, and the dance tangles amongst it all, too. The mosaic stretches between the columns, framing the threshold to the main bathing pool and guarding the path to the windowed lounge that sits beside the baths. All along the length of it, the figures dance along, beckoning the viewer to advance alongside them.

Artemisia has done with stone what paint alone cannot. Beneath their feet, the ground is more than chips and tile. It flows like the healing waters, shifting in light-shimmers and gentle tides of river-green and emerald and night-blue. She catches the glint of gold, set in to catch the water reflections, and glass, too.

"It's beautiful." She's seen it come together in parts. Seen the shattered stone in the trays, the palettes of beautiful colours waiting to be settled. It doesn't prepare her for how it looks together. "You're a wonder."

Artemisia sighs. She pushes her hair back from her face, leaving a streak of damp along her cheek. "It's done," she says, as if that's the best thing she can muster to say about it. "So that's something."

"You'll like it better with some distance."

"Perhaps. Right now, I'm rather sick of looking at it entirely." She's still at that edge-raw part of the process, where all she can see are the flaws, and she wipes the rain from her glasses with a distracted air. "I had a visit from Callowan."

"Oh? Are they still on at you about the atelier?"

"More than ever. I decided to do it."

Harriet grins. "Good. They were right, you know. Your work is good enough that you should establish yourself as an atelier."

"I don't like working with others," she says, a little sour. "Except you. I would work with you over and over, Harry. I only ever want to work with you."

"I certainly have enough ideas," admits Harriet. "I've been hoping you might want to do another project together."

"Let's open the atelier together." It's said in a rush, as if she has to get it out all in one or she'll never manage to say it at all. "You and I. We can do shop fittings and pavilions. Murals and thresholds and such. We'd do it well, Harriet. We'd work so well together."

The wind rattles the plum trees outside the hall door. A few early blossoms drift in with a draught of springs-steam. Harriet blinks. "Together?"

"We'll have to come up with a name, I suppose. And take an apprentice on, eventually. It all seems far less dreary to think of doing it alongside one another, rather than alone. Say yes?"

Harriet looks down at the mosaic. The figures in it are smiling, dancing amongst the tangled border of river herbs and flowers. It's more handsome than her mural ever was.

Each tiny piece of stone, unremarkable until Artemisia found the perfect place for it.

"That's quite a proposition," Harriet says, warmth welling up through her. "I'd be a fool to refuse."

"It's good, then, that you're not a fool," Artemisia says, and kisses her.

She shouldn't, not here. It's not proper to do so where anyone might glance over and see them. But the steam drifts past, and she does. Her kiss is as gentle as the rain, and all around them, the mist sits tucked against the trees like a quilt around lovers in the cold of the night.

WHITAKER
&FINCH
NEW STUDIO OPENING
48 · Elwe street
FINEST · MURALS · MOSAICS
UNIQUE & MOST DESIRABLE
RIVERLINE   FESTIVE   ROMANTIC   IDYLLIC

An Extra Chapter

Harriet is hiding behind a shelf. It is a handsomely built shelf, piled with neat trays of ceramic and stone and precious minerals in all the stunning colours, and it makes an excellent shield.

"There you are," Artemisia says, sliding in beside her. She's a little flushed, though whether that is from an uplifted mood or a glass too-many of celebratory wine, Harriet can't begin to tell. "Hiding again? Your brother is looking for you."

Harriet peeks through the shelves. It is the grand opening of their new atelier, and the studio is full and loud with people who have come to celebrate their success. That had been baffling to Harriet, that there were so many. She'd already been halfway to overwhelmed by it. And then the reason for Harriet's hiding away had arrived.

"My *brother*—" she starts, and then immediately must cut her words off sharp, because Rowan is there, poking his head over Artemisia's.

"Yes?" he says, face bright with amusement. "This *is* cosy back here, isn't it? What a convenient little alcove." He shuffles in, so the three of them are huddled in the space. He wrinkles his nose, no doubt at the stone dust and linseed smell, and brushes something from Harriet's collar. "It's a lovely studio, Harry. A bit of a blank canvas, though. You might hang some art."

"It's a workshop, not a parlour," she says. "It'll be full of half-finished work before too long, and then you'll have your colour."

"Of course it will. You're going to be the talk of the town."

"If we are, it'll be your fault."

Rowan's laugh is as pretty as birdsong. Harriet is quite sure he's practiced it, diligently and at length. He used to laugh like he'd been kicked in the chest by a cart pony.

"I really can't fathom what you mean," he says. "You're both Gardens' artisans now. It only makes sense that he'd take an interest in you."

She should have known Rowan was up to mischief when he'd turned up dressed like he was off to an evening party, floating out of a Gardens' carriage drenched over with amber beads and silk. And then the Casca heir had climbed out behind him, and Harriet had fled to hide behind a pillar, and had been hiding ever since.

She'd spent the last hour keeping the crowd between her and Casca. It hasn't been hard, exactly, because the crowd is thick and enthusiastic. The room is full of all the artisan friends Artemisia and she have between them, and Colette is there, too, eyeing Artemisia's mosaics with interest. And, of course, Rowan and Casca, and the other nightingales that flitted in behind them. How many nightingales could fit in a carriage, anyhow?

Rowan grins at her, the amber beads in his ears catching the light. "Are you shy, Harry?"

"I am not. I'm only taking a moment to settle my thoughts."

"Entirely sensible," says an unfamiliar voice. It is a voice like moonlight and silk. "This *is* cosy, isn't it?" Madoc Casca melts into the alcove like a magic trick, helping himself to the little pocket of space at Rowan's shoulder. "You must be Harriet. I have heard so much about you."

Rowan is grinning wide enough that he's at risk of it sliding right off his face. Harriet gives him a look that promises if the room wasn't full of her peers and betters, she'd be pinching his ear about now.

Madoc Casca has eyes like Artemisia's most expensive river-green tile, and a face that Harriet thinks should be gracing a novel cover. He hardly looks like something real, dressed in draping velvet with gold drops at his ears. He makes Rowan look *plain*.

When Casca holds out his forearm for a familiar Eskan greeting, Harriet clasps it in a daze. She's too strung out on nerves to be thinking anything sensible, and so it takes her by surprise when he tugs her in and presses a kiss to her cheek.

No one, other than Rowan, has ever greeted her in such a way. She gets a face full of his intoxicating perfume, like candles and spring water, and he smiles at her shock.

"Rowan is a dear friend of mine. I hope we'll be friends, too." Then he releases her and turns to Artemisia. "I think we've met in passing, Artisan Whitaker."

"We have," says Artemisia, and gods, she's gone as cool as the winter Lune. "You are an unexpected blessing on our studio opening."

Casca only seems amused at Artemisia's stiffness. "I expect I'll see grand things from you both. Mosaics and bathing go together rather well, don't you think?"

Better than four grown people squeezed into a dust-filled alcove, is Harriet's thought. Her head is spinning a little, because the only thing keeping Casca's velvet jacket from brushing against the ruinous dust of Artemisia's tile-trays is her own body, and she's sure that both her and Artemisia combined couldn't pay for replacing fabric so fine.

"So," says Casca, leaning against Rowan's shoulder. "Who are we hiding from?"

Harriet gives her brother a panicked look. Artemisia tamps down on a smile. Rowan clears his throat.

"Ah." Casca grins, unconcerned. "Me. Well, that makes this awkward, doesn't it?"

"I wasn't hiding," says Harriet, rallying. "It's only that I found the crowds overwhelming."

Casca's face says he's not buying a moment of it, but he doesn't do her insult of saying so. He only nods, quite grave, and the effect is almost complete except for the spark of bright amusement in his eyes. "Clever of you, to build such an effective hiding spot into your studio plan."

"Not so effective," she says. "Since you found me."

He laughs, and she realises who Rowan has modelled his manners on. Madoc's laugh is *perfected*. "And I must leave again, quite swiftly, because the Society Papers have arrived."

"He's not allowed his face in the papers," Rowan says, in answer to Artemisia's confused expression. "Lady Casca is quite firm on it. But what a coup, Harry, having the papers arrive!"

"You're not leaving me to deal with them?"

"He isn't." Madoc cuts in smoothly, raising a hand at Rowan's protest. "No, you stay. The rest of us can make an escape. Go charm the papers and make sure your lovely sister's opening makes the prime pages tomorrow." He smiles at Harriet. "It was a brief but undeniable pleasure, Harriet. Whitaker."

When he leaves, the alcove seems twice as large as it was before. Harriet slams her hand into her brother's chest.

"You might have warned me!"

Rowan is laughing. "I'd apologise for him, but he's rather a law to himself."

"I can't believe you brought him to our studio opening," Harriet says. "You insufferable *weasel*."

"Honestly, Harriet." Artemisia leans against the wall. "You acted like you were going to be eaten alive."

"And you were about as welcoming as a wasp's nest."

"He was too familiar, for a stranger." She leans over to tuck a curl of Harriet's hair behind her ear. "Though we certainly will be the talk of all the artisan circles, after that showing. Never let it be said that you don't have connections."

"Come on," Rowan says, scooping them both back into the room. Some of the fervour has bled from the crowd, now Casca and his entourage have departed. "Let's go get you in the papers."

He accomplishes his task, and then Harriet must go rescue Artemisia from the interested clients and nosy artisans ensnaring her. By the time the gathering has drizzled away, she is feeling the exhaustion right through her. Outside, the narrow street of studios and ateliers is lighting up, garlands unfurling from doorways and windows. It had seemed a good idea, somehow, to hold their opening on the same day as the Night of the Muses. Fortuitous, even.

She just hadn't accounted for how daunting the entire experience would be.

Rowan ushers the last of the stragglers from the space, shutting the oak doors behind them with a very satisfying sound. "Well," he says. He doesn't look even the slightest amount exhausted, but he's well-versed in entertaining crowds. "I'll leave you to your artisan celebrations." He glances out the window at the seething street. Already, the music is starting. "Do try to get *some* sleep tonight, would you?"

"If I stay up past midnight, it will be a miracle," Harriet says. When Rowan ducks in to give her a farewell kiss, she takes him up in a tight hug. "Thank you, Ro."

He laughs, and hugs her back, and then takes Artemisia and gives her a kiss on the cheek too. She seems startled by the affection.

"There's a bottle of wine over there, as a gift from Casca. Gardens-made. Make sure you pour a proper libation to the muses tonight."

"I promise," says Harriet, and sees him off.

When he is gone, the studio seems to sigh in quiet, tired relief. The silence swirls back from the rafters, settling into its usual haunts. It had been a delight to see the space so full of well-wishers, but she likes it best like this. Peaceful and soft. A piece of the world that is theirs, and theirs alone.

Artemisia takes out her hair comb, shaking her fingers through her tangled hair. "I'm absolutely flattened," she says. "I hate that sort of thing."

"You can't hate it too much. You're smiling."

"The smile is all for you," she says, smiling wider. "Come here."

Harriet does, winding her arms over Artemisia's shoulders, and when their mouths meet, Artemisia is as sweet as honey. The whole day, tiring and wonderful, flits from her mind and all that is left is the warmth of Artemisia against her. Her breath against Harriet's lips when she draws away. The shadow of her lashes across her cheek. When Artemisia had found her, she'd been nothing but shattered tile and broken stone, pieces of something she wasn't anymore, and Artemisia had seen nothing wrong with that. She'd shown her how even shattered pieces could be a masterpiece, if one only took the care to arrange them so.

"We should make that libation," she murmurs.

"In a moment." Artemisia tucks her face beside Harriet's, and Harriet feels the tension seep from her. "I wouldn't have done this with anyone but you," she says. "I only want to be here with you."

Harriet tugs her face back around, so they can rest their foreheads together. "And I wouldn't have been near courageous enough to try for my guild pin again, if it weren't for you."

Artemisia tugs at her collar, straightening Harriet's new guild pin. It has been hers for only a few days—the guild had been steadfast on making her wait until the year turned over before they'd allow her to have it back.

When Lady Casca ignored the guild guidelines to credit Harriet's work on the commission, the guild's response had been bitter. That hadn't stopped them accepting the work as her membership submission, though, because even if they fumed about it, the Casca name held weight.

"I do love you," says Artemisia, still running her thumb over the guild pin, even as her lovely gaze fixes on Harriet. "I don't think I've told you so clearly yet."

"I think I noticed," Harriet says, smiling. "The pieces all rather add up, don't they? I love you, too, you know."

"I do," says Artemisia, and kisses her again.

They step out, shutting the door, and Artemisia pours a generous drench of wine on the threshold as she says the invocations. But Harriet is looking at the beautiful mosaic over the lintel of the door, instead. Their names, entwined together, shimmer in stone-flecks of mist-green and winter-blue and copper.

A new studio, and a commission list as long as her arm. A shared house on Willow Isle, and their names tangled like ribbons where all of Esk can see. All the pieces that Harriet never knew she was missing until they were in her hands, and hers to have.

"Come on," she says, taking Artemisia's arm. In the darkening street, the celebrations are beginning. "Let's go please our muses."

Afterword

Thank you so much for reading this little novella. I hope it inspired and delighted you.

Join my newsletter and follow along for more cosy, queer stories set in the world of Esk.

www.theahawthorne.com/newsletter

Acknowledgments

Thank you to my partner, who read this too many times and held my hand through all my doubts, and to my dear friends who never stop cheering me on. And thank you to everyone who has read this far. I hope your tea is always the perfect temperature, and you never lose a biscuit when you dip it.

About the Author

Thea Hawthorne writes queer, cosy fantasy from her home in Tasmania, Australia, always with a cup of tea close to hand. She enjoys rainy days, both in books and in real life, and will always talk about the weather. In her books, you'll find a delightful blend of found family, folklore, quiet pursuits, a lot of warmth and a little dash of steaminess.

www.theahawthorne.com

Also by Thea Hawthorne

THE MUSES OF ESK SERIES

The Muse of Missing Pieces

A Reverie of Roses

THE RIVERSENT SERIES

All Woven With Ivy

Learn More...

9 781763 861800

Shattered SOULS

Soul Weavers Series

Soul Resurrection (Soul Weavers Duology Book One)
Souls United (Soul Weavers Duology Book Two)
Shattered Souls (A Soul Weavers Novella)

Shattered Souls

A SOUL WEAVERS NOVELLA

CHANTELLE LAMBERT

Identifiers:
ISBN-13: 978-1-7635490-2-9 (paperback)
ISBN-13: 978-1-7635490-1-2 (e-book)

Available in paperback and e-book.

Book Cover Design by
Creya-tive Book Cover Design
www.creya-tive.com

*To my daughter who fills my heart with joy and love every day,
continues to be my motivation for living, and whose laughter is
my favourite sound in the world.*

I love you my precious daughter, Leearna.

Ice Mounthin Isle
Point Ice Twin Towers
Fort Mindir
Tyron
Kora
Lake Oric
Igor Mountains
Plymort
Point West

NORTH TOWER POINT
MYRDREYA
THE RIDGE PASS
MOUNT SEASIDE
MORVIK
ELVANOR FOREST
NIRDRA
DARK CASTLE
SOUTH TOWER POINT
ZALINDOR

One

STARING OUT MY rain-stricken bedroom window in the darkness, all I could hear was my parents arguing downstairs. It wasn't unusual. It occurred every week, and every week it was the same argument. Me.

There's a glass city called Myrdreya; a city my mother wanted to move us to. She told me the city was a safe-zone for people like us — Soul Weavers. My father didn't want to move. He believed we were in no danger and wanted us to live a relatively normal life with the non-magic humans.

"We're not normal!" my mother's frustrated voice trailed up the stairs.

"Doesn't mean we can't try to be," my father's voice followed.

"Our son needs the training they can provide."

Little did they know I had been training on my own for months now. Dazed, I watched the droplets cry on my window. Even the rain couldn't drown out their yelling. I outstretched my hand, flexing my fingers. Purple swirls of electricity sparked from my fingertips. The magic grew as it engulfed my hand; a ball of energy rotated in my palm. My eyes were locked on it, mesmerised by my own power.

Out of the corner of my eye, in the pouring rain, something bright caught my attention. Releasing the energy back into my body, I dropped to the floor and peered out the window. By the enormous tree in our backyard, a swirling silver portal had appeared. My parents had told me about portals, but I had never seen one before — until now.

I stared as a man stepped out of the portal. His sleek black hair hung around his shoulders, a long black trench coat trailed behind him as he walked forward. The portal faded and disappeared behind him. He moved as though the rain didn't even bother him. Whoever this man was, he didn't look friendly. Careful to keep low to the ground, I scurried across my bedroom and quietly opened my door.

My parents' arguing reached my ears again as I hurried down the stairs. I leapt off the second-last stair and ran into the kitchen where their voices were coming from.

"There's a Soul Weaver in our backyard." I said.

They stopped mid-sentence and stared at me.

"Get down," my father whispered, pushing my mother toward me.

We bent down and huddled behind the kitchen bench. None of us were combat trained; if this Soul Weaver was here to hurt us, we wouldn't stand a chance. Panic arose in my chest. My heart thumped behind my ribs as my mother held onto my arm.

"Mum, we have to get out of here."

She put a finger to her lips to shush me.

"Mum, please, I don't think—."

A blast came from the back of the house, drowning out my words. I looked up to see my father sprawled on the floor. He rolled over, pushing himself back to his feet.

"Lucas, why?" I heard my father say.

Lucas? Why would my father's friend attack us? My eyebrows pulled together as I watched my father defend himself from another spell.

"Because we can't live amongst humans. We don't belong with them. And you..." Lucas spat, "you want to live in peace with them?"

"There's nothing wrong with living with the humans, they know nothing about us," my father took a careful step forward.

A burst of wind with a silver energy ball flew past the bench and hit my father in the chest. Blasted off his feet, he immediately went out of our line of sight.

"DAD!" I stood and yelled.

Oops. There goes our hiding place. My mother tugged on the hem of my pants, I discreetly gestured to her with my hand to stay down. Lucas glared at me.

"Ah, Kieran. Is your mother here too?" he glanced around the room.

I shook my head. "No, she's working late tonight."

He stared at me silently, and I wondered if he had called my bluff. My mother let go of my clothing and I stepped forward to get out of her reach. The last thing I wanted was her to be in danger too.

"Stop right there." Lucas growled.

I paused and glanced at my father's body lying on the floor, unmoving.

"He's fine, just knocked out," Lucas folded his arms across his chest. "So, Kieran, tell me, how much magic training have you had?"

"I know enough," I eyed him suspiciously; strange question to ask.

His mouth twisted into a smirk, "in other words, no formal training. Did your parents keep you from learning the ways of Soul Weavers?"

I shifted on my feet, forcing myself to not turn to look at my mother. Swallowing, I ground my teeth as I thought over his words. My mother wanted me to go to Myrdreya, to not only be safe but to train. My father had other plans.

"Come with me, and I will teach you everything I know." Lucas said, stepping toward me. "You're what... sixteen?"

"Fifteen." I corrected.

He nodded, "right, close enough. Join me, Kieran, and I will teach you everything your parents never did."

My heartbeat thumped in my ears. My chest tightened as I glanced from my father to Lucas. I didn't dare glance at my mother.

"I'm fine, thank you. I can learn on my own."

"Very well..." Lucas's voice changed. "You leave me no choice then..."

My mother didn't allow him to finish. She jumped out of her hiding place and threw her hand out in front of her. A royal-blue energy ball instantly left her palm and stopped in front of me. It grew larger, filling the space in between Lucas and I, shielding me from him.

I took a step back. The shield followed me like a magnet. Another royal-blue ball flew past me; this time it hit Lucas square in the face.

"You lying little—."

He didn't get his words out. Another ball hit him; this time it was bright-green. I turned to find my father standing with his feet apart and a hand outstretched in front. His expression was determined.

"HOW DARE YOU!" my father yelled.

Lucas's eyes dashed from me to my mother and father before he turned and bolted away. Three against one—the odds were not in his favour. My father bounded through the kitchen after him. I swiftly followed him out into the backyard. We stood side by side staring at the space before us; Lucas was gone.

WITH NO SIGN of Lucas for two weeks, my father deemed us safe again. My mother wasn't convinced, and neither was I. I was constantly feeling like we were being watched. *What were they waiting for?*

My mother had secretly started training me, without my father knowing. He didn't want us to bring attention to our magic while living with the humans—*but what was the point in being a Soul Weaver then?*

A purple ball of energy shot out of my hand and hit the back door window, shattering it. I cast a quick glance at my mother, who was instantly casting a spell, her focus on the door. The shattered pieces of glass lifted from the ground and reformed together again as if it hadn't happened.

"Amazing. Imagine if we could just fix things for regular humans like that?" I joked.

"Then the world would be a more peaceful place." She said.

I stared at the sadness in her eyes for a moment.

"Why didn't we just portal to Myrdreya?" I asked my mother while my father was at the shop.

"You can't just portal into Myrdreya uninvited, you have to be escorted there. The shield around the city will throw us off the edge of the island the moment we portal in." She replied. "While your father is..."

"Stubborn?"

"Yes, stubborn... it's unlikely we will get there." She said.

I frowned. "Where is Myrdreya exactly?"

"It's high in the sky." She smiled.

"An island in the sky?" I raised my eyebrows.

She nodded. "The most beautiful city you would ever see."

I imagined a floating island high in the sky, made of solid glass. A key turned in the lock on the front door and my father walked in a moment later. My mother grabbed the dishcloth and pretended she had just finished cleaning the kitchen.

"Hey, dad." I greeted.

He raised his eyebrows, "odd to see you down here."

"I was just getting a drink." I lied.

I followed his eyes to my mother, who had just rinsed the cloth and hung it on the tap.

She turned and smiled, "honey, did you remember the milk?"

"Of course," he nodded as he stepped forward and placed the bag of groceries on the kitchen bench.

I slipped away upstairs, back to my bedroom before my father could ask me anything else. I closed my bedroom door to shut out their chatter; I wanted to avoid being around when they argued again.

Stunning colours of the sunset shone through my window. It was like the sky was on fire. The particles in the atmosphere were changing the directions of the light rays beautifully this afternoon. Somehow the phenomenon was so calming; I flopped down on my bed and allowed my worries to float away with the light.

⁂

EYES OPENING WITH a snap, I quickly realised it wasn't my eyes snapping—it was something else downstairs. I quietly climbed out of bed and froze. A loud bang sounded through the walls and floor. The blood left my face, dread washing over me.

Bolting for my bedroom door, I pulled it open and dashed down the hallway toward my parent's bedroom. I didn't quite make it to their room when my father stepped out. He grabbed my arm and pulled me into the room behind him, closing the door quietly.

"We should have left when we had the chance." I heard my mother whisper.

I searched the room for her; I hadn't been in my parent's room for what felt like years. It still looked the same; dark wooden king-size bed with a blue-patterned bedspread. Matching bedside tables sat on either side, topped with a black lamp. My mother crouched beside the bed, near the beside table.

My father ignored her comment and turned to me, "let's portal out of here before—."

The bedroom door blasted inward, smashing my father in the back. I jumped backwards as the sound of my mother's cry erupted around the room. My father fell forward, slamming to the ground with the door.

With his blue eyes and a goatee that matched his short trimmed dark-brown hair, I stared in horror at the man standing before us. My eyes widened as I stretched my hand out in front and cast a shield spell in the doorway, shielding us from the man. I glanced over to my mother; it was thanks to her that I knew how. Her eyes were locked on my father's; he reached a hand toward her.

"You know what to do," he hushed to her.

She nodded and looked directly at me. I stared at the man in the doorway; he thrust his hand against the shield. My father reached his hand forward and thrust a shield up in the doorway, his bright-green magic replacing my violet, just in time when my shield collapsed.

"Kieran, come," my mother pulled herself up, holding her hand out toward me.

We couldn't possibly be leaving without my father, could we? I lifted the door off my father, pushing it to the side. He shook his head.

"No, leave me." He muttered.

A blast of orange light hit my father's shield — I stared wide-eyed at the man trying to break through. Reluctantly, I ran over to my mother, leaving my father on the floor, blood dripping from his head.

A portal appeared in the ensuite behind me, its royal-blue glow was illuminating the bedroom. I glanced at my mother, her hand was still outstretched.

"Quickly, into the portal." She said.

"No, mum, you're coming with me."

"Of course, after you," she glanced at my father.

"GO!" my father yelled just as an orange spell hit him, silencing him.

My mother pushed me toward the portal.

"No — wait — Dad —"

"No time," my mother said frantically. "Kieran, we love you."

I looked over my shoulder, frowning. Before I could utter a single word, she shoved me into the portal.

DARKNESS. All I could see was the black forest I now stood in. I whipped around, observing my surroundings. I was alone with no reminiscence of my mother's portal. The realisation that my mother hadn't made it through the portal hit me. My heart pounded heavily in my chest, my breathing uneven.

My father had sacrificed himself in an attempt my mother and I would get away. He had never been supportive of me learning how to be a Soul Weaver, but his sacrifice in the end somehow made up for it. But, my mother wasn't here. *Did she not make it to the portal? Had she taken a different portal? Had she never intended on coming with me?* I should have grabbed her hand and pulled her through with me. I should have learnt how to protect her.

I collapsed against a tree trunk, staring ahead at the

dark trees in front of me. With no idea where I was or what to do now, I leaned my head back on the bark. I was thankful it was a warm night; otherwise, the shirt and shorts I wore wouldn't be ideal and my bare feet would be frozen. Without any breeze, an owl hooting nearby, and no moon shafts through the canopy, it was very eerie.

After what seemed like hours of sitting on the dirty forest floor, I willed myself to move. I walked through the trees with no idea where I was going. Glancing up into the canopy, I searched for any sign of direction; but there was nothing except thick leaves.

A branch snapped nearby. I whipped my head around wildly, searching the dark trees. I moved my feet faster; anxiety growing. With still no clue where I was or where to go, I hoped I was traveling in the right direction. *Was there ever going to be an end to this forest?*

Kicking my toe, I leant forward to grasp it, but I hit my forehead. I stared ahead, frozen in place. Lifting my hand, palm flat and facing away from my body, I slowly stretched out to touch the air. My hand flattened in midair — on an invisible wall.

Eyes widening, my heart pounding behind my ribs, I touched the invisible wall with both hands. It felt like glass, yet I couldn't see anything there. I ran my hands up and down it; it went all the way to the ground and higher than I could reach. I spun around toward the direction I had come and reached out. My hands hit another wall. I didn't understand. *How did I walk through one wall but not through the other?*

Turning my head, I looked to either side of me. I stretched my arms out from the sides of my body, but I didn't fully stretch out before I hit two more invisible walls. Dread washed over me. I was trapped in an invisible square cage. I punched my fist on the wall in front of me — I was instantly thrown backwards and slammed into the opposite wall. I groaned as I stretched my back out.

A bush nearby rustled, and another branch broke. I stared in the sound's direction, squinting through the darkness.

"Who's there?" I called.

A youthful woman dropped from a nearby tree; she landed lightly on her feet as if she had floated down. My mouth hung open as I stared at her.

"Clara is my name," she ran her fingers through her short purple and black hair as she stepped forward.

I eyed her up and down. Long black boots covered her feet, black tights hugged her legs, and a long loose dark-green top covered her torso with a studded belt around on her hips.

"I'm—"

"I know who you are." She interrupted.

I stared into her amber eyes, "how do you know me?"

"I was at your house, took longer than expected to find you."

I stumbled backward and hit the invisible wall behind me.

"You were with that man who attacked us?"

Her brow furrowed, "no, but sounds like you can describe him."

I glanced at a tree behind her, lost in thought about the appearance of that man. He had been no older than my parents.

"My parents... are they okay?" I asked.

She held up a hand toward me, yellow energy erupted from her hand. I swallowed, staring at the magic sweeping from her palm. It swirled and licked at the invisible wall for a moment, and then it evaporated.

"Come, you have much to discuss." She stated.

My eyebrows twitched as I looked around.

"You can move now," she said, shrugging, "can never be too cautious."

I nodded, understanding. Stepping forward, the air in front of me was clear again.

"Where are we going?"

"Myrdreya."

My mother spoke of the glass city often—maybe she had been right all along. Suspended high in the sky, the floating glass island had been created hundreds of years ago. They designed it to train us how to use and control our magic, and to provide us safety in a cruel world.

Clara's hand erupted with yellow energy again as she reached toward a nearby tree. The magic swirled and grew into an oval-shaped portal. I stared at the mesmerising gateway to the city; I could barely discern a glass bridge in the yellow.

"After you," Clara said, gesturing her hand toward it.

Swallowing, I stepped forward. I took a breath and stepped through. As I stepped out of the portal, the sun rays peeped between the clouds, shining upon the glass city before me. Myrdreya—finally.

Two

"WE KNEW YOU would come one day." Clara said, her amber eyes glowed with the purple and black framing her face.

I blinked. "My parents…"

"What happened?" Clara's face fell and she looked over my body. "You've got no belongings with you. You left in a hurry."

It wasn't a question. Knowing was plastered on her face. I swallowed awkwardly.

"How do you know me?" I asked, staring in awe at the city behind the girl standing in front of me.

"Your mother," she explained, stepping closer to me. "She sent word to us a week ago that you had been attacked and to be ready to greet you in the case of you appearing. But…we thought your parents would be with you."

I took my eyes away from the glass view and focused on the girl. She looked me up and down again, lingering on my bare feet.

"You were attacked at home?" her eyes snapped back to mine.

I gave her a curt nod. She turned and waved over a guard who stood metres away.

"Send word to Demetri, Kaylee and Lance are in trouble, they were attacked at their house."

The guard, dressed in black and grey, hurried away.

Clara held out a hand to me, reaching for my shoulder. "Come on, you need to get cleaned up and rest. I'll show you to your room. You're safe here."

"No." I shook my head, planting my feet shoulder width apart. "I have to see my parents. Are they still alive?"

"I don't know," she dropped her head and looked down, avoiding my gaze.

"Send me back. I have to see."

"I can't," she said, her head hanging. "Your mother gave us specific instructions to not allow you to return."

"I don't give a shit about her instructions," I glared at her. "If they are dead, I have to see it to believe it."

The girl gaped at me, her mouth hanging open for only a moment before she bit her lip.

I sighed. "Please, if you were in my position, you

would want to see too."

She searched my face, her eyes flickering between mine as she chewed her lip, before she finally spoke. "Fine. But, we must be quick. I'll get Jake."

"Who's Jake?"

"You'll see."

She left me standing on the glass platform connected to the city. My eyes drifted around the city and across to the edge of the platform I was standing on. Myrdreya — a city made of pure glass by ancient Soul Weavers thousands of years ago, suspended high in the sky above a secret island — Zalindor. I never imagined being here alone.

I stepped toward the edge of the platform and looked down. Nothing but clouds in sight. I stared at the fluffy white for a long moment.

"Not going to jump, are you?" a man's voice sounded behind me and I jumped back from the edge, fixing my wide eyes on him.

A smirk played at his mouth. His dark skin and dark brown eyes, along with his bulky figure would be daunting to most people who didn't know him, but not to me. I stared at him.

"No." I said bluntly.

Clara stood beside him, petite in comparison. "This is Jake."

"We better make this quick before Demetri knows we're gone." Jake said. "Come on, to the portal room."

Jake and Clara led me through Myrdreya to an almost

empty room, except for two young women standing together. One of them stepped forward, her white blonde hair swaying behind her as she embraced Jake—a pure contrast of dark and light together. Jake ducked his head to meet her lips and I turned away, facing the other girl.

"Hi, I'm Mae," she cheerfully said before turning her back to me and stretching her hand out in front of her.

After never seeing a portal in my life, I had seen three portals in the space of hours. I stared into it; a fuzzy image of my laundry discernible.

"How do you know where I live?" I asked, my eyes not leaving the portal.

"We know a lot more than you think," the white haired girl said, drawing my attention to her. "I'm Tori. Nice to finally meet you, Kieran."

My brows furrowed as I looked between Tori, Jake and Clara. I blinked and shook my head. "Okay, let's get this over with."

Tori and Jake stepped forward, their hands interlocked. Clara stood beside me.

"We'll go first. Walk on through after and Clara will follow," Tori said as she and Jake moved forward as one and disappeared through the swirling portal.

Clara gave me an encouraging nod before I stepped forward. My feet lifted from the solid ground and a swirl of colours surrounded me. I held my eyes open watching the array of colours shift around me for what felt like minutes before they arranged themselves into my laundry. I stood in the middle of the small tiled room,

Tori and Jake were standing by the door, their eyes wide.

"What—?" I began, but Clara clamped a hand over my mouth.

When had she arrived? I hadn't even seen her appear next to me. She put a finger to her mouth and I nodded. She released me and I stayed silent upon her command. We listened to voices that drifted down the stairway.

"He got away," a deep man's voice grunted.

"Spot the fucking obvious, dipshit," another man's voice snickered.

"What are we going to tell Julianne?" the first voice said.

"We tell her they're dead, but the boy escaped," a third voice chimed in—this one clearly female, and sounded very young. *A teenager? But, I couldn't focus on that—my mind reeled on her words. My parents were dead.*

"We need to find him. She must have sent him to Myrdreya," the man with the deep voice said.

There was a long moment of silence before the other man spoke. "Why are you here if you are just going to state what we know? Work on a plan to get him back."

My heart pounded in my chest, breathing becoming heavy. Clara glanced at me and mouthed *I'm sorry.* I tore my eyes from her and crossed the room. I gripped the door handle and pulled it wide open before any of them stopped me.

"What are you doing?" Tori urgently whispered.

"Get back here!" Jake hissed, reaching out to grab my shirt.

I jumped out of his reach and ran up the stairs, taking two at a time. When I got to the top landing, three pairs of eyes locked on me, surprise etched into their faces.

"Looks like we don't have to look far," the girl snapped — she was barely a teenager, her raven black hair draping long down her back, icy-blue eyes boring into mine.

"Well, well, well," the deep voice said, "come back to die with your parents?"

My jaw flexed and I stared at them. Footsteps rushed up behind me, Jake grabbed my shoulders and shoved me back behind him. Clara gripped my wrist and pulled me to her. I twisted my arm but she held onto me tight.

"You will not take another life today, Jay." Jake spat the name like it was poison.

The red haired man smirked and threw up his hand. Magic licked out of his fingers, forming a shield, the same orange tone I had seen earlier when he had entered my parent's bedroom. The girl formed a ruby red portal behind the shield and the other man escaped through it immediately. She turned her gaze on us and threw fireballs at us. We ducked back down the stairs, the fireballs narrowly missing us. I glimpsed over the rim of the upper stair just in time to watch them dive into the portal and vanish.

My eyes drifted from the vacant hallway to my parent's bedroom, the door stood ajar. They didn't stop me when I climbed the stairs, bolted down the hall, and into the room. I stopped short and stared at the two unmoving bodies. My mother's hand lay outstretched toward my father's. Blood pooled around her skull, her hair wet and glossy. I couldn't take my eyes away from her open lifeless ones.

No tears shed. My blood boiled up under my skin, threatening to seep out every pore of my body.

That red haired man had murdered my parents, along with his comrades. Jay. My parent's murderer's name was Jay—and I was going to seek revenge and kill him.

Three

I WALKED SILENTLY through the glass city, following Jake and Tori. Clara walked beside me. Tori glanced over her shoulder, casting a sly smile my way before turning away again.

"I'm sorry about your parents," Clara said, placing a hand on my shoulder.

I had the urge to shake off her hand—I didn't know these people, and they knew more about me than I thought possible.

They led me to the middle of the floating city, to the tallest tower. We strolled up the spiralling ramp and when we reached the top, a man with white hair and emerald green eyes stood waiting—his expression hard and unforgiving.

"Here we go..." Clara said under her breath.

I frowned, glimpsing her wary expression before fixating on the man.

"So, whose idea was it to take him back into the danger that his mother just got him to escape from?" his voice was stern as he eyed us all.

"Mine." Clara swallowed.

I frowned. "No, it was mine. I made them take me."

The man's jaw twitched as he studied my face. "Hmm."

He turned and walked through the doorway that stood ajar behind him. Jake and Tori followed him without hesitation. Clara raised her eyebrows and moved forward to follow them. I walked up the remaining of the ramp and entered the room—it looked like an office, but with portraits covering the walls.

"Previous leaders of the council," the man's voice drifted across the room and I snapped my eyes to him.

He was watching me intently. Tori and Jake stood together to the right of the room, and Clara stood by the doorway.

"Please," the man opened his hand and gestured to the chair in front of the desk, "sit. We have much to discuss."

"How do you know who I am?" I asked, ignoring the invitation to sit.

The man pursed his lips and seated himself behind the desk, his hands clasped in front of him on the wooden tabletop.

"My name is Demetri." He said. "We're here to help Soul Weavers. Your mother was a loyal member of the council, until she married your father and he wanted nothing to do with us."

I swallowed, crossing my arms. "My father has never been here, and my mother has never lived here."

"No, he hasn't," Demetri shook his head. "But, your mother has. She lived here for many years, until she met your father on a mission. He refused the offer to move here to be in safety. Unfortunately, his friend ratted him out to the wrong people. Julianne and Jay had been looking for your mother for some time, and his friend led them right to her...right to you."

"Who are Julianne and Jay? Why did they want my parents dead?" I asked.

"They are Dark Soul Weavers. Kaylee went on a mission with Julianne and Kaylee betrayed her. Julianne almost lost her life, but she did lose her a child. She blamed Kaylee for her child's death, so she wanted revenge to take you from her," Demetri watched me closely. "But, instead, your parents paid that price because your mother ported you away before they could get to you."

I adverted my eyes to the ground. My parents died because the murderers didn't get to kill me. My mother was no traitor, she couldn't have betrayed Julianne— *could she?*

"Kieran, I'm sorry for your loss. Losing both your

parents and then being brought here can't be easy." He said. "If there is anything we can do to make your grief easier, please let us know."

"A proper burial." I whispered.

"Pardon?" Demetri asked.

My eyes found his again and I watched him as I said, "a funeral for my parents."

After a long, silent moment, Demetri nodded.

Clara squeezed my wrist and stepped forward to Demetri. "I've already asked for their bodies to be brought back here. We can have an ash ceremony tomorrow."

Demetri bucked his lips and nodded. "Alright, I'll leave it to you to organise it, Clara."

Clara nodded and she looked over at Tori and Jake briefly before turning to me. "I'll show you to your room."

⁂

CLARA OPENED A thick, clouded glass door to the biggest bedroom I'd ever seen. My mother hadn't been lying when she told me all about everything being made of glass—the furniture, the walls, the doors, and the transparent roof.

"Magnificent, isn't it?" Clara said.

I nodded. "Yeah."

She pulled the curtains open and pushed the glass doors ajar to reveal a balcony overlooking the city. I gaped at the view, my mouth hanging slightly open.

"This is your home now," she said, a hand resting on the balcony rail.

I stepped out and leaned on the balcony. "How long have you lived here for?"

"My whole life."

I raised my eyebrows. "Really?"

She smiled. "Yes. My parents met here and had me. My father was unfortunately killed during a riot a few years ago and my mother..." her voice trailed off, the smile gone.

"Is she...gone too?"

She nodded. "She killed herself a few weeks after losing my father."

"I'm sorry." I whispered, keeping my eyes ahead.

She shook her head. "Don't be. It is what it is. Can't change the past, can only learn from it. Demetri has mostly taken care of me. Jake and Tori are great friends too. I'm sure you'll become great friends with them as well."

I sighed, watching the white fluff shift slowly through the sky. Clara cleared her throat and walked back inside—I followed her.

"I'll let you rest and get used to your surroundings," she said as she crossed the room to the entry. "The wardrobe is already equiped with clothing and you'll find the shoes will fit you as well. Your mother had everything prepared incase."

I swallowed, a small, but sad smile playing at the

corner of my mouth. My mother really had organised everything for me incase the worst was to happen.

"I'll have someone bring you some food in a bit."

"Thank you." I said, offering her a smile.

Clara gave me a quick nod and closed the door quietly as she left. I took a deep breath and let it out slowly. My parents were gone and I had the names of their murders. I had a whole room set up for me, a whole life here that my mother had prepared for me.

She had always hoped that one day we would move here, but I don't think she had planned for me to be here without her — totally and utterly alone.

Four

T HE GREAT BURNING star lit up the sky in an array of oranges, reds and blues as it slowly descended. I stood with my hands clasped behind my back, my eyes watching the sun sink lower, only an hour after I had set my parent's ashes free over the edge of the city. Clara had set up a small, but beautiful, memorial—more than I could have asked for.

No tears fell. Numbness succumbed me, enveloping my skin and bones. Stars gradually started twinkling, filling the sky with what looked like millions of fireflies, drawing my attention to them. *When had it grown dark?* I blinked and looked around me in a daze. Everyone had dispersed, leaving me alone at the edge of the city—

everyone, except Jake.

He sat metres from me, leaning his elbows on his knees, looking out at the night sky as well.

"I never get sick of watching the sunset and the stars." Jake's deep voice drifted over to me.

I swallowed, tearing my eyes away from him back to the twinkling starlights.

"Each star could be a soul that had once lived, watching down on us." Jake said. "Every friend we lost. Every parent. Always there."

I chewed my cheek, my brows raising. *Was he delusional?*

Jake huffed. "Of course, they are just balls of hot gas, but I like to think our loved ones are watching over us."

Oh, not delusional — just making odd conversation? I rubbed a hand over my neck.

Jake pushed himself up and stepped closer to me. He didn't tower over me, but he was taller. His dark skin made my sun-kissed skin look pale as he stood next to me.

"Tomorrow morning I was going to practise magic, did you want to join me?" Jake asked.

I peered over at him out of the corner of my eye. "Ah, yeah, that sounds good."

"Cool."

We stood in silence, watching the sky turn from shades of purple to deep blue to black. It was easy to stand quiet with Jake — like there was no expectation of conversation without the awkwardness.

SWEAT POOLED ON my brow. Standing with my feet wide, I held my hand outstretched in front of me.

"Your mother taught you well," Jake said as I blocked yet another of his lime-green fireballs.

I nodded. "Yeah."

I adverted my eyes, gazing around the training room. Others trained in pairs or groups, far more advanced than me. They probably grew up here though; training since they could talk, no doubt.

"Hey," Jake strolled over to me and placed a hand on my shoulder, "you should be proud of what your mother taught you. If it wasn't for her, you would be starting from scratch."

I nodded absentmindedly, my eyes on a pair to the right—one was Tori, the other was a younger girl. Tori's magic hit the girl square in the chest and blasted her backward. She jogged over to her and helped her to her feet.

"Have you used a dagger before?"

The question brought my attention back to Jake, my eyebrows furrowing. "No."

"Well, then," Jake grinned, whipping a sheathed dagger out from his deep pocket, "let's start."

He held the small package out to me—my eyes darted between the dark purple leather and Jake.

"For you." Jake raised his eyebrows.

I took the dagger and gripped the black handle, pulling it from its sheath. The violet blade stunned me and I paused, staring at the talon-shaped metal attached to the black hilt in my hand. Intricate lined patterns ran along the middle down to the sharp point.

"This..." my mouth gapped, "is mine?"

Jake smirked, crossing his arms over his chest. "Yep. Your mother had it made for you years ago. Purple to match your magic. She gave it to me to hold for you until you were old enough."

My eyes lifted to his. "Thank you."

Jake inclined his head. "Let's see what you can do with it. Clip the sheath to your belt."

I turned the sheath over; eyeing the clip, I flicked it with my thumb before moving to clip it to the belt at my hip. With my other hand free now, I inspected the blade closer. Tiny writing entwined in the pattern caught my attention—the words *Love Mum* in an elegant font. My lips turned up at the corners; one last gift left for me from her.

"She's beautiful isn't she?" Jake said.

I raised my eyebrows, staring at him. "What?"

"Your blade. Her name is Shadowtalon."

"Daggers have names? I thought that was fantasy."

Jake laughed. "If you hadn't noticed, we're technically what non-magic would call 'in a fantasy world.'"

I rolled my eyes. "Yeah, I guess so."

"Come on, show me what you got," Jake unsheathed

his own dagger and flipped it in his hand, parting his legs in a battle stance.

I gripped Shadowtalon and eyed Jake. "All right, let's do this."

Jake jutted forward, hooking his arm around, the blade coming close to my cheek before I leaned backward away from harm. I side stepped, forcing him to do the same to keep me in front of him. Thrusting my dagger forward, Jake avoided my blow with expertise.

Readjusting Shadowtalon in my hand so that the hilt was upside-down in my palm, blade pointing toward Jake, I side stepped again. Hooking my arm around, like Jake had done earlier, the blade soared toward his upper arm. Jake jerked his arm backward, but the curled tip of my blade caught his shirt and tore a hole in it. Jake glanced down at his sleeve.

I shrugged. "Oops."

Jake grinned, jumping forward. I twisted away from him, but he turned and thrust his dagger forward, catching me off guard, his blade tearing through material and flesh.

I hissed at the wound down my thigh, bracing it with my hands. Blood trickled through my fingers and tainted the glass floor.

"First battle wound." Jake chuckled. "You all right?"

I looked down at my bloodied hand. "Um, yeah, I think so."

Jake lunged at me with his blade. I jumped backward.

"Woah!" I said as I gripped the dagger in my hand.

"In a battle, there's no time to weep over a wound."
Jake said and he sliced his dagger down toward my arm.

I ducked and side stepped. "Fair call."

I hooked my blade toward his upper thigh, but he
rolled away from it easily. The wound in my leg was
barely noticeable as I jumped forward and sliced at his
hand. Jake swung his dagger as he stepped in a circle
around me and jabbed toward my uninjured leg. The tip
of his blade scraped my pants, ripping a hole; thankfully
not touching my skin. He may be more skilled, but I was
younger, smaller, and more agile than him.

"Hope you weren't attached to those." Jake taunted.

"Got plenty of them." I retorted, spinning away with
my dagger slashing out beside me in attempt to catch
him off guard.

Jake's hand gripped around my wrist and squeezed.
I dropped my dagger. Shadowtalon skidded across the
ground and I spread my arms out wide, palms facing
forward.

"Well, I don't think you have plenty of daggers,
though." Jake joked, wiping his own dagger clean on his
pants.

I rolled my eyes and bent over to inspect the damage
on my thigh. I pulled the tear open and stared at the
dried blood.

"What the?" Jake muttered as he stepped forward
staring at my skin.

I grazed my fingertips through the dried blood,
scraping it away — the wound was gone. I had a deep cut,

I know I had. The blood was the telltale sign it had been there.

"Did you…heal yourself?" Jake asked, his expression blank.

I blinked. "No. I can't heal."

Jake reached out and checked the non-existent wound, running his hand over my skin as if I was hiding the cut. He straightened and eyed me. "Are you sure?"

"I've never healed myself before." I said.

He frowned. "Get your dagger. Let's go visit the city's healer."

I raised my eyebrows briefly before ducking to pluck Shadowtalon from the ground. Jake was already strolling out the entrance of the training grounds once I had turned back to him. I hurried to catch up, falling into step with him as we walked a short distance to a small building next to the training grounds. I sheathed my dagger and picked at the blood under my nails.

Jake rapped on the door and I dropped my hands to my side. Mere seconds later, the door swung open revealing a petite girl with a long scar running the length of her right arm. Her ebony hair was cut into a short asymmetrical haircut, falling over the sides of her face.

"Elle, are you busy?" Jake asked.

The girl turned her dark blue eyes upon me, tilting her head. She gazed over me, eyes stopping on my thigh.

"Have you got a wound?" she asked.

"He *had* a wound." Jake said, crossing his arms.

She frowned and then stepped aside, waving a hand

to indicate us to enter. Jake inclined his head and I walked through the doorway; he followed me into the building and the girl closed the door behind us.

"Sit," she pointed to a chair across the room, "let me take a look."

My eyes scanned the small room as I crossed it and seated myself—it was like a doctor's office, but not. There was another door opposite the entrance, a cabinet full of vials of who knows what in them, a desk and chair, a bed, and the chair I seated myself in. There wasn't much else.

"So, you must be Kieran. I'm Elle, the city's healer," her eyes bore into mine as she moved to crouch in front of me.

"Nice to meet you." I said.

She smiled and gazed down at my thigh. Her tiny delicate fingers touched my skin—poking and prodding. After a moment she stood, moving over to the desk where she opened a packet and pulled out a small cloth. She returned to me and placed the damp cloth on my skin, wiping away the remaining of the blood.

"We were training with daggers," Jake explained, leaning on the wall by the entry door, "and I sliced into his thigh. There was a fair amount of blood. Not long after, the wound was gone."

Elle nodded, tossing the bloody cloth into a trash bin and standing.

"So, you're a healer." Elle said.

"Um, maybe? I mean, I didn't know I was one." I said, leaning back in the chair.

"Healing gifts often awaken during late teen years or even into young adulthood. You healed yourself completely, no scarring at all." Elle grinned, her thin eyebrows rising up her forehead. "That's impressive. Especially when you've never done it before — or not that you know of anyway."

My brows furrowed. "What do you mean?"

"Well, you might have had very minor bruises or hair-string cuts that you didn't even know you got in the first place, and they've healed."

"Wow," I gaped at her, "that's amazing. Will all my wounds heal like this?"

She shook her head. "No, like all magic, it'll have its limitations. I can heal minor to mild wounds and sicknesses. Herbs aid me to heal as well. Other healers have been known to bring people back from the brink of death, but those healers seem to be very rare."

I nodded. "Right. So, what about my healing ability?"

"We won't really know what you're capable of until you have the chance to act upon it. You'll find your limitation over time, sometimes it can take many years." Elle explained, leaning a hand onto the desk. "It can depend greatly on the type of wound. If the wound is from magic itself, it will scar. Magic wounds can be healed, and it depends on how bad it is to how much of a scar is left."

"Magic is pretty incredible." I raised my eyebrows. "So, I guess I wait for someone to hurt themselves and then I can try heal them? But, how? What do I do?"

Elle grinned. "That's the beauty about healing. All you have to do is concentrate and place your hand near the wound. Your gift will do the rest."

"It's that easy?" I frowned.

Elle shrugged. "Sort of. You still have to have the right amount of concentration to heal someone else. Whereas, healing yourself is just automatic."

"It's a pretty rare gift." Jake said, drawing my attention to him.

"Do you have a gift?"

Jake nodded. "Yes, I can tell if someone is lying."

"Wow. I bet that's useful."

His lips pressed together into a hard line. "To a point. It can be difficult to read people. I'm still learning how it works."

"My mum told me there were gifts, but she didn't go into details about them." I said, my eyes shifting to the floor. "Did they have gifts?"

"No, they didn't," Jake pushed off the wall. "But, even if they had, it was unlikely they would have escaped."

I nodded, keeping my eyes to the ground. He knew exactly where my thoughts had been going.

Five

THREE MONTHS HAD passed and I had learnt an abundance of skills. Jake had been tirelessly training me in the use of daggers, short swords, defensive magic and some simple offensive magic. Thanks to my mother, I had already learnt how to use magic in my mind, casting without saying the words out loud. Jake had been quite surprised by this, but it had made the training easier for him.

Jake had been away on a mission the past few days, so I had been wandering aimlessly around the city and trying to practise my skills on my own.

One afternoon I was about to enter the training grounds when Clara called my name. I spun around and gazed upon the turquoise up-do she wore; her bangs bouncing as she bounded over to me.

"Hey Kieran." She said.

"Hey," I pointed at her hair, "changed your colour again, I see."

"Every month."

"Right," I dropped my hand. "I was just heading to train."

"Well, that'll have to wait. Demetri wants to see us." Clara flicked her hair out of her face with her fingers. "Come on."

"What about?" I asked.

She shrugged and turned in the direction of Demetri's tower. "Don't know, but best to not keep him waiting."

I followed Clara in silence. I was a bit awkward with her in silence—unlike how natural and peaceful the quiet was with Jake.

We entered the room and stood side by side in front of Demetri.

Demetri leant forward on his desk. "The day your parents died—."

"Murdered." I cut in, my voice sharp.

Demetri's eyes flicked to Clara momentarily; he took a breath before speaking again.

"The man you identified with the shield, that was Jay. He and his wife Julianne left us years ago and turned dark."

I frowned. "What do you mean?"

"Dark Soul Weavers." Clara answered. "They use

their magic for bad things."

"They have a daughter," Demetri said, barely noticing Clara had spoken at all. "Her name is Trixie. They abandoned her when she was a young child, but we've found her."

"Okay." I said, shifting on my feet.

Demetri's emerald eyes bore into mine. "We need to watch her house."

"What do you want with her?" I swallowed.

"We need to know more about her, and if she shows any signs of magic you must inform me immediately."

"Wait, me?" I spat, my fists clenched at my side. "Why me? Her parents killed mine."

"We might be able to save her from her parents. If she has magic, they will want her back." Demetri said.

I shook my head, grinding my teeth. "Someone else can't watch her? Why me?"

"Jake and Tori will be tied up looking for Jay and Julianne. Others have their own assignments as well." Demetri leaned back into his chair. "You're young, so she won't see you as a threat if she sees you. Clara will be watching your back in the forest."

"I will?" Clara asked.

"Yes. You're a good spy. You can watch Kieran stays out of trouble." Demetri said.

She crossed her arms and shrugged. I glanced at her out of the corner of my eye. She didn't seem annoyed by Demetri's decision—if she was, she was covering it well.

Crunch.

"Shh," Clara hissed beside me. "You're going the right way to get caught."

I lifted my foot carefully off the broken stick. "Well, I'm the last person that should be doing this."

"I agree," she said, and I looked over at her, "you shouldn't be here."

"So, is that why you're annoyed to babysit me?"

"No," she frowned. "And I'm not babysitting. I'm your backup. You know, in case you're attacked or Trixie is attacked, I'm here to drop in and help."

"So, you're not just here to make sure I don't do something stupid," I stepped forward through the forest, watching my foot placement to avoid more stick snapping.

"Look, I'm not annoyed at being here with you. Don't take it personally," Clara said. "I'm annoyed because I know how unbelievably boring this is going to be."

"Oh." I sighed.

We trudged through the forest, the glow from the streetlights growing brighter as we neared.

"Her house is just up here," Clara whispered. "When we get there, we need to scout the area. I'll scout from the trees, you sneak around her yard, checking windows and doors for tampering."

"Okay."

"Kieran," Clara stopped walking; we were only

metres from the edge of the forest, "do not let her or anyone else see you, unless her life is in danger. Understand?"

I nodded. "Got it."

"Right, off you go then," Clara pointed toward a grey house, only a few houses up. "Go in from the back so no one sees you on the street. I'll be around. I'll let you know when it's time to go home," Clara turned her back on me, and I turned toward the house Clara pointed out to me.

I strolled past a couple of houses before I reached the grey house, an owl hooted somewhere in the forest and some kind of rodent scurried across the lawn as the wind picked up around me.

I crept around the house, my senses on high alert. The night air was cool against my skin, and the only sound was the gentle rustling of leaves in the breeze. I checked each door and window, my heart pounding in my chest as I searched for any signs of tampering or intrusion. Nothing.

I gave the forest trees a thumbs up — where Clara hid, somewhere. I would have looked crazy from an outsider, or from Trixie if she caught me, and I had no idea if Clara had actually seen me.

As I made my way to the backyard, I couldn't shake the feeling of unease that had settled in the pit of my stomach. The irony of the situation wasn't lost on me — here I was, protecting the daughter of the people who had murdered my parents. *What was I doing? I shouldn't be here.*

Spotting a bushy tree outside the dining room window, I climbed. Climbing trees was my favourite thing to do as a kid; even broke my arm and leg once from falling out of one. But, that had never stopped me going back up massive trees.

The branches were rough against my palms as I hoisted myself up, my muscles contorting as I manoeuvred myself. I settled myself in a fork half way up the tree, letting out a frustrated sigh, my grip tightening on the bark.

"Of all the people, I have to watch over her," I grumbled to myself, my voice barely audible over the rustling of the leaves. "The universe sure has a twisted sense of humour."

With a deep breath, I scanned the surroundings, my eyes searching for any signs of movement in the shadows. The night stretched on, and I settled in for a long watch, my mind filled with conflicting emotions. *What if this girl was the same one at my house? What if she had been involved in all this?* My stomach churned and bile rose. I closed my eyes and swallowed it down, taking a deep breath.

My head tilted as darkness took me — I was falling.

Falling, falling, falling.

An endless black hole stretched out below as my body continued to fall.

"Oi," a hand shook my shoulders and my head jerked upward.

My eyes snapped open and I refocused on the

surrounding leaves and the branch I was perched on. Glancing to my right, Clara gripped the tree trunk, leaning toward me.

Clara raised her eyebrows. "Sleeping on the job, are we?"

"No—"

"Sure…" Clara rolled her eyes, shifting backward, lowering herself on the next branch over.

I shook the memories of the dream away, and eyed the window closest to the tree. "Sorry. Had I missed anything?"

"No. And, don't worry about it. This is your first time, you'll get better at staying awake the more watches you do."

"How long do we have to do this?" I asked, looking over my shoulder at her.

Clara sighed, running a petite hand through her bright hair. "For as long as she's unsafe from her own parents."

I stared at her; her eyes were off in the distance, probably watching the house like I should be. Her hair was so vibrant.

"Do you always wear your hair so brightly coloured?"

"No one will see me up here, if that's what you're concerned about."

"No," I shook my head. "You just always have the brightest, craziest hair."

She grinned, her amber eyes twinkling as she gazed

over at me. "I like to be different. Everyone is boring with their brown or blonde hair. I like to stand out and be…me."

I raised my eyebrows. "Well, you definitely stand out. I am surprised no one can see you up here."

"The leaves are thick enough, unless someone stands below and looks up, we're both unseen."

I nodded, glancing down. We were a fair way up the tree, but she was right, anyone could see us from below, if only they looked up. Most mundanes don't look up, though.

As the hours ticked by, I found myself growing increasingly restless. My legs cramped from the uncomfortable position, and my mind wandered, drifting between memories of my parents and the frustration of my current situation. It was a constant battle to stay focused.

I found myself fighting the urge to doze off, my eyelids growing heavy with each passing minute. Clara would pinch me hard, the sharp pain jolting me back to alertness. I would grumble, shooting her a disgruntled expression, before scanning the surrounding area between the leaves.

"While we're out here, you can learn to heighten your senses," Clara whispered. When I looked at her, frowning, she continued, "you need to learn to listen to your surroundings and see off into the distance where otherwise you wouldn't be able to."

"Right…"

"I'm serious. Close your eyes and listen to all the sounds you can hear. When you hear something interesting, focus on that sound." Clara explained.

I took a breath and did as she said. Closing my eyes, I lent my head back against the bark. The rustling of the leaves around us was all I could hear.

"So, what can you hear?" Clara asked.

"Wind."

"What else?"

"The leaves in the wind."

"Kieran," Clara groaned. "Listen further away from this tree. Think about the road out the front of the house, are there any cars, people, dog's barking, bird's chirping, water running?"

I frowned. "No."

"You'll have to try harder. I can hear a car driving up the road, there's a bird chirping about twenty metres away as well, it sounds hungry like it's a baby waiting for its mother."

"Seriously?" I said, opening my eyes and turning to her.

She nodded. "Yes. With practice, you'll be able to hear it too—oh, someone just turned a tap on."

"Really?" I raised my eyebrows, straining to listen through the sound of the gust blasting through the leaves.

"Practise it every time you're out here just waiting for something to happen. It makes it a bit more interesting, rather than just sitting here bored out of your brains."

"You can say that again," I mumbled.

"Well, otherwise, you can jump down and do a parameter check," Clara whispered. "It's probably time to do another scout."

I nodded. "Okay."

After carefully scouting the backyard and declaring it clear, I climbed down the trunk, my feet landing softly on the grass. I scampered across the yard and pressed my back against the wall of the house, making my way toward her bedroom window.

Leaning forward, I placed my hands on the window seal and peered through the window, my breath fogging up the glass as I tried to get a better look at Trixie through the gap in the curtain. She was sprawled out on her bed, her blonde hair fanned out around her. In the dim light of her bedside lamp, her face looked peaceful, almost angelic. She was definitely not the girl from my house.

Trixie stirred, and I ducked, my heart pounding in my chest. *Had she seen me? Would she scream for help, thinking I was some kind of creep?* After long a moment, I peered back over the window seal. I let out a sigh. She merely rolled over, mumbling something incoherent before drifting back to sleep.

ONE YEAR LATER

Six

I GRITTED MY teeth, my muscles burning with exertion. Over the past year, these training sessions had become a lifeline, a way to channel my grief and anger into something productive. With each passing day, my skills grew sharper, my reflexes quicker. Daggers were definitely my weapon of choice, but lately we were using swords; Jake said I had to learn to use as many different weapons as I could so I was able to pick up anything to use as a weapon if I needed. Makes sense really.

Clutching the hilt, my hand resting against the cross-guard, I ducked and swerved to the right, spinning out of my opponent's reach, his blade narrowly missing my torso. Jake jumped forward, slicing downward and I met his sword with my own.

Jake chuckled. "You're getting better."

"I know I am." I said smugly, drawing my sword back and thrusting forward.

Jake spun sideways, but my blade nicked his arm and a hiss escaped his lips. "Nice one."

"Maybe better than you."

"Hey, don't get ahead of yourself. I tripped you yesterday and could have cut your throat."

I shrugged. "Yes, well, it happens to the best of us." I sighed. "I was thinking about my mother. I wish she could have seen how good I'm becoming."

Jake rested the tip of his blade on the ground and leant on the black hilt. "And she would be proud."

The corner of my mouth twitched.

"Are you boys still at it?"

Tori flicked her long blonde hair over her shoulder and pranced across the room into Jake's arms. His hand released the sword and it clattered to the ground, adding more scratches into the glass surface. He embraced Tori, holding her firmly around her waist and resting his forehead on hers, nudging her nose with his own. I took my eyes off them as Clara entered the training grounds, shaking her head. I raised my eyebrows at her.

"Those two are inseparable." Clara said. "I thought you and Jake were bad."

I scrunched up my face. "I don't skip around and leap onto him like that."

"Are you sure you two don't have a secret friends with benefits thing going on? I mean, I've never seen you with a girl."

"I'm definitely straight if that's what you're asking."

She pursed her lips. "Hmm."

Jake turned his head away from Tori, a smirk growing on his face. "He wouldn't be able to handle me."

Tori giggled and twisted around in Jake's arms, facing forward, her back against his torso. "If only you were straight too, Clara, then you two could date."

I laughed and Clara punched my arm.

"He wouldn't be my type even if I were." Clara said.

We all laughed together; a regular occurrence these days. In an originally awful situation, they made my life more manageable.

"Anyway," Clara turned to me, "Demetri has a mission for us."

"Back to the daughter's house?" I mumbled.

"Nope."

I raised my eyebrows. "Oh? Where to this time?"

"Back into your neighbourhood," Clara said. "Soul Hunter chasing time."

"My mother told me about Soul Hunters. They think we're an abomination, right?"

Clara pursed her lips. "Something like that," she said, crossing her arms. "But, we're not. So, let's go find out what they're up to. You can wear what you're wearing, bring your dagger. Meet me at the portal room in about half hour."

"Oh, right, we're going today." I handed the sword to Jake. "Alright, see you in thirty."

⚜

Our feet landed on pavement in front of a familiar abandoned building. Broken windows and crumbling walls loomed before Clara and I. Stepping forward, we skirted around the walls down an alleyway leading to a maze of decaying structures.

Our footsteps echoed too loudly on the cracked pavement as we stepped over the overgrown vines snaking across the path. Long shadows stretched between the stone as twilight ascended. The air tasted like rust, leaving a metal taste in my mouth.

Pressing myself against a moss-slick wall, I peered into the gloom of the warehouse before us. A cavernous maw of shadows stretched the length of the ruined building, casting shapes on the abandoned crates and rusted machinery. Squinting, I peered out the gloomy window closest to me. Nothing appeared to be moving.

"Kieran? Anything?" Clara whispered into the eerie stillness.

"Nada. You?" I whispered back.

"Nothing yet."

We prowled deeper into the gloom, eyes straining against the disappearing sunlight. The only sound was the soft scuff of our boots and the thundering of my own heartbeat.

Sweat trickled down my spine as I wove between the detritus of forgotten machinery. I couldn't shake the feeling of being watched, of unseen eyes tracking my every move. My fingers tightened around the dagger on my belt.

A flicker of light caught my eye and I froze, turning my head sharply toward it. Half-hidden by the mountains of crates, a rusty door stood slightly ajar, a faint glow seeping from the cracks.

"Clara," I hissed. "Look."

Hardly a heartbeat passed before she materialised at my side, eyes sharp and wary. She followed my gaze to the door. We shared a glance, silent understanding passing between us. I stepped forward, attempting to be light on my feet; Clara trailed closely behind me.

"If there's anything video games have taught me, it's that doors lead to treasure or death," I whispered over my shoulder.

A laugh bubbled up her throat. "Kieran, I swear to God, if you get me killed down there, I will haunt you for eternity."

"Let's hope for treasure then."

The air grew dank as we moved carefully toward the only source of light left in the warehouse. I met Clara's eyes, seeing my own grim resolve reflected back at me.

No turning back now.

A chill raced down my spine as the air around us grew colder. Water dripped somewhere in the distance, each plink echoing through the old building. My hand touched the handle, and with one last breath, I pulled the door open.

The dim lighting beyond met our faces as we peered through the doorway at a hallway stretching on for what looked like twenty metres or so before it sloped downwards. The dim light emitted from a single lantern hanging on the wall by the entry.

I swallowed, my mouth turning dry. Clara looked over her shoulder, browsing the warehouse for any spies, I assumed.

We crept forward, our footsteps muffled by the earthen floor, the cement of the warehouse changed to dirt. It grew denser and darker, the light now far behind us. We stayed close together, our daggers gripped in our hands, as we began the decent downwards.

We plunged into the abyss—relying only on our own breathing and senses to find our way through the tunnel. It twisted and turned, stretching on for what felt like an hour, disorienting us. The deeper we went, the more my skin crawled with the sense of being watched. *No one could be watching us, though, could they?* Our senses told us there was no one nearby.

"How long does this go on for?" Clara whispered somewhere from my left.

A hand touched my left shoulder. I flinched.

"It's just me." Clara said. "I don't want to lose you in this darkness."

I let out a whoosh of breath as her other hand held onto my right shoulder. "Of course, sorry. This tunnel is giving me the heebie-jeebies."

"Yeah, me too."

Time stretched on as we stepped down another set of stairs, our footsteps scuffing lightly on the dirt. My hand touched yet another curve in the wall, and we turned toward the right. A dim light came into view; another lantern illuminating a door—ancient wood reinforced with bars of tarnished metal.

"Oh, finally," Clara sighed, I felt her hand slide off my left shoulder.

"What do you think is behind there?" I queried; I eyed the door through narrowed eyes as we approached.

"A secret society of Soul Hunters...maybe?" Clara said too casually.

"Right, why don't we just open it and go in blind?" I said sarcastically.

We stopped a metre from the door, a faint yellow glow emitting from beneath it. Clara still held onto my right shoulder—I shrugged, giving her the hint to let go. She didn't.

"Do you need to still be holding onto me when we can see each other now?" I murmured.

"I'm not."

I looked at her sideways, both her hands hung down at her sides, her dagger gripped in her right. My eyes met hers for a moment before we both spun around.

"Surprise!"

Seven

Y BLOOD TURNED to ice. Clara and I whipped our daggers up in front, facing our purser. My eyes darted to his hands—one held up after releasing my shoulder, the other hung loosely at his side. No weapon.

"How long have you been following us?" Clara asked, her voice turning cold.

The man's voice was even colder, and gruff. "For as long as he felt *your* hand on both his shoulders."

"And, who are you?" I spat, shaking off the fact his hand had been holding my shoulder that entire time.

His lips curled at one side without answering me.

A click sounded behind us, a creak of metal, and we

turned as the door opened revealing a woman with sandy blonde hair cut to her shoulders. She froze and blinked, taking in the scene before her. After a brief acknowledgment of the daggers in our hands, her eyes widened and her fingers reached for her own hidden dagger.

Clara acted immediately, jumping forward, jabbing her blade toward the woman. A gasp left the woman's mouth as the metal pierced her flesh in her thigh. Her fingers dropped her dagger she barely managed to unsheathe. Clara grabbed her arm, turning her around, holding her blade against the woman's throat.

"Don't move a muscle," Clara breathed into her ear.

The man sneered. "Impressive, I like a strong woman."

Clara made a gagging sound; if it wasn't for the situation, I would have laughed.

I rolled my eyes at the man and showed him my blade. "Would you still be impressed if she slit your throat?"

The man appeared to be considering my words. "Don't know. I wouldn't be alive to say."

"Funny," I said, taking a step closer to him. "How about you and little miss here keep your mouths shut and we'll be on our way?"

"Ha!" the man said, "you two wouldn't make it out of the tunnel."

"I wouldn't be so sure, we're pretty fast." Clara teased.

He raised his eyebrows. "That, I believe…but, this kid here," he gestured to me with his chin, "would stumble and fall."

"I'm better on my feet than you think," I said, readjusting my grip on the dagger.

The man lunged, his movements a blur. I dodged the blow, my fist connecting with the Soul Hunter's jaw instead.

The man stumbled back, his eyes narrowing. "You'll pay for that," he snarled.

He charged again, his fists flying in front of me. I ducked and weaved, my movements fluid from the training Jake had been giving me. I circled around, my eyes searching for an opening.

I jabbed the dagger forward, but he side stepped my attack easily. He laughed as I struck again; and again, I missed. I groaned as his fists clashed with my jaw, knocking me sideways.

"You're weak, kid," he said, "you can't beat a full grown—."

I ducked down, kicking my leg in an arc, knocking his legs out from under him. He slammed to the dirt floor with a growl.

I stood over him. "How's this for weak?"

I flipped the dagger around in my hand, bent down and slammed the hilt into the side of his head. His eyes rolled into the back of his head. Knocked out cold.

I looked over at Clara—the woman was lying at her feet, knocked out, too.

We stood there for a moment, our chests heaving. The tunnel was silent, save for the sound of our ragged breathing.

"Come on, let's move them into here and hide them," Clara said, bending down to reach under the woman's arms.

Dragging our attackers through the door, their feet making trails in the compressed dirt tunnel, we briefly assessed the room we had entered. The stone mouldy walls met with the cracked stone flooring; a pile of crates in the far left corner of the tiny room, and a hallway opposite to us, leading off into the next room where the yellow light emitted from.

Clara pulled the woman behind the large stack of crates, and I followed suit. I stepped back to check they couldn't be seen unless you were looking for them; Clara retreated back into the tunnel, scuffing up the trails their feet had made. Clara nodded and jutted her chin toward the hallway when she returned.

Keeping our footsteps light, we crept into the hallway. Walking only metres, it opened out into a large room, filled with more piles of crates around the edges, a round wooden table in the centre that would accommodate about ten people, if not for the lack of chairs. Gazing around the room, I eyed the crates and the table.

"No one here?" I said.

Clara shook her head. "No, looks like they were alo—."

Clara dragged me behind a stack of dusty crates. My

heart hammered against my ribs as footsteps grew louder, closer, echoing off the stone walls like the beating of a war drum.

"Stay down," she breathed, pressing herself flat against the cold floor.

I nodded, following her movement and flattening myself on the floor next to her, barely daring to breathe, as the footsteps reached the doorway. I strained my ears, trying to catch every word.

"…can't believe she wants us to hit that target next," a gruff voice said, tinged with annoyance. "It's too well-guarded. We'll never get in and out alive."

"You questioning orders?" a second voice snapped, cold as the grave. "She knows what she's doing. If she says we strike, we strike. End of story."

The first voice grumbled, but I didn't catch what he said.

A rustling of paper, the scrape of boots on stone, reached my ears. My muscles tensed, ready to fight or flee at a moment's notice.

"Look at this," the second voice said, a note of grim satisfaction in his tone. "She's mapped it out."

A map. I glanced at Clara, saw my own curiosity mirrored in her eyes. We had to get that map. Had to find out what the Soul Hunters were planning.

Footsteps sounded from the hallway. Between the thin gaps of the crates, our eyes flickered over to the entryway. A girl with long black hair entered, pursing her lips — the same girl from my house.

My heart hammered behind my ribs, my hands balling into fists. Clara must have sensed my fury; she placed a hand over mine, gripping it with so much intensity I looked at her. She shook her head, and mouthed what I thought was 'don't.' Clenching my jaw, my breathing quickened, as I refocused on the three others in the room.

"Hello, boys," the girl's cunning voice lingered in the air as the men stepped back, allowing her a clear path to the table. "Shall we—where are the other two?"

The men shrugged, gazing at one another momentarily. I swallowed and glanced sideways at Clara. We could only hope they stayed knocked out for long enough so we could escape.

The girl sighed. "Well, I'll be having a word to them when they reappear. Let's get moving, I'd like to be home by morning."

One of the men folded the map and tucked it into his pocket. *Shit.*

The girl turned on her heel and lead them back out of the room. "I just need to stop by the old building on Lenox Street, I'll meet you at the X."

The footsteps started to recede, the voices fading as they moved back through the tunnel. I let out a shaky breath, my muscles unclenching.

"That was close," I whispered, my mind racing.

Clara nodded. "Too close. We need to get out of here."

"They took the map. What do we do now?"

"Return to Demetri," she said. "Tell him about the old

building on Lenox Street. I think we should get back up and check out the building."

Slowly, carefully, we crept out from behind the crates.

"Come on," Clara said, her voice low and urgent. "Let's go."

We made our way back through the darkness, our footsteps quick and quiet. My heart pounded in my chest, adrenaline coursing through my veins.

As we reached the exit of the tunnel, I paused, glancing back over my shoulder. The tunnel stretched out behind us, dark and silent. A shiver ran down my spine.

WE BURST INTO Demetri's office, our bodies still thrumming with adrenaline. He looked up from his desk, his brow furrowed with concern.

"What happened?" he asked, rising to his feet.

The words tumbled out of me, a torrential flood. "We found the Soul Hunters' hideout. In the abandoned warehouses. There was a hidden tunnel system, and a map."

Demetri's eyes widened, his expression grave, his fingers steepled beneath his chin. "What kind of map?"

"We don't know, we didn't get to see it," Clara said.

"But, the girl, the one that was at my house, she was there," I said, my breath coming out in heavy puffs. "She's heading to Lenox Street right now and we think we should go check it out."

Demetri nodded, crossing his arms. "Yes, I agree."

"Are Tori and Jake back from their mission?" Clara asked.

"I believe they got back an hour ago. Good thinking, take them with you."

Clara and I raced out of Demetri's room.

Eight

THE OLD BUILDING'S flickering torches cast an eerie glow over us as we trekked soundlessly through the corridors. My heart pounded in my chest, as I clutched my dagger in my right hand. Something rotten reached my nostrils, and I scrunched up my nose.

If we succeeded today, we would be one step closer to getting revenge on my parents' murder. This young girl, whoever she was, could be the key to finding Julianne and Jay—if we can get her to talk. She's just a child, of course she would break and tell us anything we wanted to know. *Wouldn't she?*

We crept around a corner after Jake indicated to us it

was safe, and came to a rusty old metal gate. With his sword in one hand, Jake pushed on the gate and we all tensed.

CREEEEAAAAK.

"Jesus, could you be any louder?" Clara whispered.

"Jesus ain't here." I muttered.

Clara glared back at me. Jake's mouth quirked up at the side as he turned away, clearly trying to hide a grin.

I shrugged. "Sorry, couldn't help myself."

Clara rolled her eyes and stepped through the opening. Jake, Tori and I followed Clara down the next hallway.

"How do we know she's here?" I whispered.

"We don't." Jake answered.

"Right."

"Less talk boys," Clara muttered.

"She's right," Tori said. "We want the element of surprise."

Silence followed Tori's words as we crept down the hall. A scrapping sound reached our ears, causing us to pause. Tori nodded at Jake and he peered around the corner. I clutched Shadowtalon in my palm, ready to strike if the moment should arise.

Jake leaned back, glancing at Tori and whispering, "someone is in the room to the left."

Clara and I leaned in closer to be able to hear them.

"Alright, on 3." Tori whispered back.

I held Shadowtalon tighter, swallowing.

"1, 2," Jake counted. "3."

The four of us rushed around the corner and into the room to the left. I stayed close to Clara. We stopped and stared ahead. My gaze swept the room; ancient dim metal lanterns lined the mouldy stone walls and the black haired girl stood in the middle of the small room.

"It's over," Tori declared, her amber eyes blazing with determination. "You can't run from us any longer."

The girl's lips curled into a wicked smile. "Oh, who said anything about running?"

Jake tightened his grip on his sword, the leather of his jacket rustling. "Come quietly, and we won't hurt you."

I glanced at Clara, her colourful hair shimmering in the dim light, as she stepped forward. "What's your name, little one?"

"Little one?" the girl's voice sounded disgusted as she rolled her eyes. "You've got no idea, do you?"

Tori stepped forward, her hands crackling with energy. "Come on, don't make this harder than it needs to be."

"But, where's the fun in that?" she cackled, turning her back and running out the opposite door I hadn't noticed before. *Damn it.*

Jake and Tori rushed forward, trailing the young girl. Clara and I followed behind. We hurried down a hall which opened out into a stone courtyard. Stone benches lined the walls. Archways taller than the surrounding walls, stood in a hexagon formation, ivy leaves growing their way up and down the pillars. Metal fences with intricate swirl and leaf designs connected every second gap of the pillars together.

The girl stopped in the centre of the courtyard and turned to face us. Jake and Tori skirted around the edges, standing on either side of her, Clara and I stood in front where we had entered. Tori stepped sideways, rounding toward the back, blocking another doorway.

"So," the girl said, her eyes following our movements, "how are we going to this? Blades? No blades? Magic?"

A kind of hatred boiled through my blood as I stared at her, but I was bewildered that such a youngling could harm my parents. *Had she really been a part of it? Or, maybe she had been forced?* She hadn't looked scared at my house, and she didn't look scared now. *Was she really just pure evil?*

"Hmm," her eyes found mine, "you're Kieran, right? Pity your parents had to die, although, you were supposed to die with them."

I gritted my teeth. *Yes, pure evil.*

"Oh, well, I shall fix that," she smiled, her teeth showing.

"Enough, girl, you're out numbered." Jake said.

The girl sighed. "No, not really." She raised her hands, ruby red tendrils of fire escaped her fingertips and grew into a swirling ball of fire. She let the fireball loose, bolting toward, not me, but Clara.

I blinked. I spun to check on Clara. She ducked and threw her own yellow fireball back toward the girl, but it missed as she spun away from it, laughing. Her laughter sent chills down my spine. I jumped behind the closest pillar, peering around it, looking for an advantage point.

The girl was fast, conjuring fireball after fireball, while dodging the orbs being thrown back at her from all angles. Yellow, lime green and white orbs crossed over as they hurtled toward the girl. She sent a flurry of ruby red back toward them; she didn't miss any of their movements, staying one step ahead of them. I stepped out, Shadowtalon at the ready, and my other hand raised.

I threw a violet fireball toward her; she ducked and rolled toward me. I slashed the dagger out as she neared me, but the blade missed. Her elbow clashed with my cheekbone, throwing my head sideways.

I groaned as my skull slammed into the archway on my right—the place I had been hiding behind a moment before. A sword sliced through the air, sending the girls stumbling backward. I gave Jake a quick nod as I rubbed the side of my side—my hand came away sticky.

Wiping my blood on my pants, I looked over my shoulder. The girl's hands were spread wide, a ring of ruby red fire surrounding her. Her grin was malice as she pushed a blast of fire toward Jake.

"NO." Tori's voice cut through my bones, deafening us.

Everything happened so fast. One second Jake was standing there with his sword in hand as a large fireball soared toward his torso, next second the stone and metal from next to me warped in front of him. The fireball hit the stone and dissipated.

Tori's eyes widened in horror and Jake cried out. I

reeled around and stared at the blood dripping from his stomach and the metal protruding from it. Jake dropped to his knees as the gate tore through his flesh, releasing from his body. He fell forward in a pool of his own blood.

"Jake!" Tori screamed, her voice raw with anguish. She rushed to his side, her hands trembling.

I couldn't do anything but watch in horror while the girl's evil cackling laughter reached my ears. I narrowed my eyes, turning toward her, vengefulness crossing my features.

Clara moved to shield Jake and Tori, her stance defensive as she faced the powerful child.

"You think you can stop me?" The girl laughed, a chilling sound that echoed off the brick walls. "You're nothing but children."

"Pretty sure you're the only child here." I gritted my teeth, anger and fear warring within me.

"Oh, he does have a voice," she teased. "But, does he have fire resistance?"

The ring around her grew at an incredible speed. We barely blinked as it crashed through us, surrounding us and the archways. The ivy leaves caught alight, catching the archways in a blaze. Gazing over at Tori, Clara and Jake, I frowned, staring at their untouched clothing. My own clothing remained intact too.

I knelt beside Jake, my hands hovering over his wounded stomach as I focused all my energy on mending the damage the metal had caused. My heart raced, and my breath came in short gasps as I poured every ounce of my soul's strength into healing my new friend. I couldn't lose him, too.

"Stay with me, Jake," I muttered, my voice strained with the effort. "I've got you."

Jake's face contorted in pain, his skin pale and clammy. I clenched my jaw, squeezing his shoulder with what I hoped was comfort.

The air thickened. Heat scorched my back and I glanced over my shoulder. My eyes widened. The flames encircled us in a fiery ring reaching half way up the archways. Clara and Tori's expressions mirrored my own as they took in the sight of the flames.

The girl's laughter echoed through the room. "What is a weakling like you going to do?"

I gritted my teeth, refusing to let her words get to me.

The flames crept closer, the heat searing my skin; but, I ignored them and turned back to Jake. The warmth of my power flowed through my fingertips, knitting together the torn flesh and organs. The bleeding ceased, but Jake remained unmoving.

I risked a glance over my shoulder, just in time to see Clara launch herself into a series of flips and twists, her movements so fast and fluid that even the young girl seemed momentarily caught off guard. Tori joined in, her own Soul Weaver abilities creating a dazzling display of light and colour that danced around the courtyard, drawing the girl's attention away from me and Jake.

I looked over at the girl. Her eyes narrowed, lips curling into a wicked smile. With a flick of her wrist, she sent a blast of flames hurtling toward Clara and Tori, the force of the impact sending them flying backwards — over the wall of flames.

I gazed around the circle of fire. *Smart girl.* She had separated us, leaving me and Jake alone and vulnerable, cut off from the others.

"KIERAN," Tori cried out, her voice filled with panic. "Look out!"

I spun around, my heart pounding in my chest, to find a face framed in black hair standing before me, her eyes glinting with the flames. "Well, well, well," she purred, her voice as smooth as silk. "The healer, all alone. How... convenient."

I swallowed hard, my mouth dry. "I'm not afraid of you."

She threw her head back and laughed, the sound harsh and grating. "Oh, Kieran, you are exactly where I need you to be."

She reached into her jacket, pulling out a small crystal device that glowed with an eerie, pulsing light.

"Do you know what this is?" she asked, her voice thoughtful. "It's a power siphon. And it's going to drain every last drop of your precious gift."

My eyes widened, and I took an involuntary step back — the heat of the flames stung my back.

"Please," I said, my voice trembling despite my best efforts to keep it steady. "You don't have to do this."

"Oh, but I do," she said, her eyes cold and hard. "And I'm going to enjoy every moment of it."

"Kieran, keep away from her," Tori called somewhere behind me across the fire wall.

The girl raised the power siphon, her other hand reaching toward me. Searing pain ripped through my body. It was like nothing I had ever experienced before, a white-hot agony that seemed to burn through every nerve ending and every cell.

I groaned, my knees buckling beneath me as I collapsed to the ground. A part of my soul tore from me, ripped away like a bandage from a raw, open wound.

Everything around me grew hazy. I blinked once — twice. Only a blur of red, gold, orange, grey and black surrounded me.

Through the haze of pain and whirl of colours, I could hear my name being shouted, the voices desperate and afraid. I tried to open my mouth, but it wouldn't obey. I couldn't respond, couldn't even move. My eyes were the only organ that still obeyed me; so I could watch the horror of what was happening. I was helpless, trapped in a prison of my own body as this girl ripped my soul from me.

It was going to be over soon. I would die just like my parent's did — *was this how they died? Was she the one that tore their lives away from me?*

Her hands let go and I collapsed to the floor, my legs no longer able to hold me upright. The pain receded, leaving me weak and shaking on the cold, stone floor. I was wrong. She hadn't been ripping away my soul, but maybe just a piece of it. *What had she taken?*

"Poor little Kieran," she cooed, her voice dripping with false sympathy. "How does it feel, to be so weak? So...ordinary? Your gift stripped from you like your parent's were."

I groaned, lifting my head. "*You* killed my parents."

She pursed her lips. "No, that was Jay. I only watched."

Despite her not being my parents' murderer, my blood boiled for revenge. My hostility urging to break through and release the venom within me. My bones and muscles shook under me as the last ounce of strength left my body.

A cold and empty void resided where my healing gift had once been. I reached within me, searching for the warmth that I had only recently grown accustomed to—nothing.

"What have you done to me?" I ground out, barely able to keep my eyes open.

"I'm surprised you're still conscious after that ordeal," the girl stepped around me, encircling me. She flipped the crystal in her hand. "Your healing gift is mine."

I shuddered; a full body shudder that tremble through my muscles and bones.

"I couldn't let someone like you have this extraordinary gift, a weakling that doesn't deserve it."

I looked up at her through my eyelashes. "And you...do?" my words were barely a whisper.

A wicked grin spread across her face. "One day you'll

understand. Lucky Jay hadn't killed you, or I wouldn't have this awesome new gift."

She turned away. Through my blurry eyes, a ruby red portal appeared in front of her. I outstretched my hand, like I was going to stop her. She stepped through her portal and the flames disappeared along with her.

My body trembled, as the reality of what had just happened sunk in. A tiny little girl stole my healing gift; a gift I only had mere months to use was gone.

Jake.

I rolled my head to look over at my friend. He was still unmoving. I had failed.

The world seemed to be fading away, the edges of my vision growing dark and fuzzy. I allowed my eyes to close as shouts from Tori and Clara grew louder.

"Kieran," Clara cried beside me. "What has she done to you?"

Whatever was said after that I hadn't heard. The weakness overtook me and I allowed myself to succumb to the darkness.

Nine

M Y EYES FLUTTERED open, straining against the dim light filtering through the curtains.

"Kieran," Clara's voice drew my gaze to her petite frame perched on the edge of my bed. "How are you feeling?"

I attempt a grin, but it came out as more of a grimace. "Like I've been trampled by a herd of angry unicorns."

Clara bit her lip, her fingers fiddling with the frayed edge of my blanket. "Kieran, I'm so sorry."

I looked away from her, the memories of fire, metal, and my gift being stolen enveloped me. "There's nothing you could have done."

"The fire wall was too tall and," Clara's eyebrows

pulled together, "Tori, she was scared or something to use her warping gift, especially after hurting Jake."

"Jake — is he — okay?"

Clara nodded. "Yes, he's…okay."

Her hesitation had me narrowing my eyes.

"You healed him enough that he's recovering from the injuries."

"Where are Jake and Tori?" I asked, pulling back the covers and swinging my legs over the side of the mattress.

Clara's face fell, her gaze dropping to the floor. "Kieran…Tori's gone. She disappeared, and Jake…he's been locked up in his room for days, refusing to see anyone."

"Days?" I frowned. "Wait, how long have I been unconscious?"

"Five days."

I jumped to my feet. "What?"

"You used a lot of magic to heal him. Your body can only take so much, especially when magic is so new to you," she explained, twisting her body toward me. "Your mind and soul needed to sleep to regain strength. You could have killed yourself."

I nodded. "Right. Well, he would have done the same for me."

Clara stood and placed a hand on my shoulder. "I'm glad you're finally awake. It's been lonely without you and Jake…and Tori."

"Why did Tori leave?"

She shook her head. "Only Jake can answer that, but without him speaking to anyone, well, we don't know."

I took a breath and seated myself back on the edge of the bed.

"Kieran, I think perhaps he might speak to you. You saved his life, so maybe..." her voice trailed off.

"I'll go see him," I said as gurgling sounds sounded through the room.

Clara raised her eyebrows. "Maybe after you eat, though."

"Right, I suppose I need food after being asleep for five days," I smiled up at her.

⊛

Stumbling through the hallways of Myrdreya, my footsteps echoing off the glass walls, I reached Jake's room. My hand hovered toward the door, hesitating for only a moment before I knocked. No answer. I knocked again and pushed on the door, but it didn't budge.

"Jake?" I licked my lips. "It's me, Kieran."

I waited another minute before sighing and turning away. A soft click sounded behind me, and I swivelled back to the door as it opened. I swallowed, looking Jake up and down; he stood in the doorway wearing black cotton pants and a dark grey t-shirt. His eyes were...dead. He looked like hell.

He stepped aside, allowing me to enter. The curtains

were drawn tight against the outside world. I squinted, my eyes adjusting to the gloom. Jake closed the glass door behind us, plunging us further into darkness. I gazed up and saw the twinkling stars looking down on us from the sky. A light flicked on, drawing my attention away from the heavens.

Jake's face was pale, his eyes distant and unfocused, staring at the floor.

"Jake," I whisper, my voice cracking with emotion. "I heard Tori left."

Slowly, his eyes drift to mine, recognition flickering in their depths. "Kieran," he breathed, his voice hoarse from disuse. "I…I can't…"

Jake dropped onto the edge of the bed, his hands fisted in his lap.

I moved to his side, sinking down next to him. "I know, Jake. I know it hurts. But we'll find her, we'll bring Tori back home."

Jake shook his head, his eyes filling with tears. "It's my fault, I shouldn't have been in the way."

"What do you mean? In the way of what?"

"She warped that gate into me because I had been in the way."

"You can't blame yourself," I said. "And, she didn't mean to hurt you either. It was just an accident."

"She doesn't see it that way," his eyebrows pulled together. "She left because she didn't want to hurt me again. She almost killed me, and she blames herself, so she left."

I reached out, grasping his shoulder, the tension thrummed beneath his skin. "We can find her. We can get her to understand that it was just a mistake. You survived."

"Only because of you," he muttered. "But, you can't do that again, can you?"

I lowered my hand. "No." I frowned, staring down at the floor. "Tori left because I couldn't heal anymore?"

Jake shook his head. "No. She left because she couldn't stand the thought of hurting anyone again with her magic."

I sighed. "We'll find her, Jake," I bore into his saddened eyes. "I promise you."

Jake met my gaze, a flicker of hope ignited in his eyes. "You really think we can find her?"

I nodded. "I know we can."

Jake drew in a shuddering breath, his gaze drifting to the curtains, through the tears in his eyes. Slowly, he rose from the bed, his movements heavy with the weight of his grief, and he gripped the curtains pulling them open.

Jake's voice, rough and raw, broke the silence. "I kept searching for her. Every time I looked out this window, I hoped to see her walking up the path, coming back to me."

I walked over to him, placing a hand on his shoulder. "She'll come back. But, you need to come out of this room. We'll find her and bring her back. I promise."

"Thank you, Kieran," Jake released a deep breath like he was releasing built up tension.

Ten

AKE'S EYES WERE distant, unfocused, as if he were seeing something beyond the fluffy clouds that surrounded Myrdreya. The heaviness in the air around us reflected the emptiness in Jake's eyes. Since Tori's disappearance, my evenings were spent sitting with him, mostly in silence. I could see how her absence had shattered his soul, like how my parents' murder had shattered mine.

"It's been weeks," Jake whispered. "Weeks, and still no sign of her."

I nodded, my throat tight. "I know. But we'll find her, no matter how long it takes."

Jake turned, his brown eyes searching mine. "When?

When will we find her?"

"Doesn't matter when," I sighed. "It matters that it will happen. I don't know when, but I promise you, I won't stop looking."

We lapsed into silence again, each lost in our own thoughts. We'll find Tori; I didn't know when or how, but I knew we would one day find her because we won't give up.

"I've been thinking about our search," Jake said, twisting in his seat. "I have a plan."

I leaned forward, my interest piqued. "What do you have in mind?"

Jake pulled out a worn piece of paper, spreading it across the table before us—a map. "I've been studying the map, trying to think of ideas about where she might have gone." He pointed to a series of marked locations on the map.

I studied the map intently, my mind racing. "You think she might have gone to one of these towns?"

Jake nodded, his gaze fixed on the map. "Yeah, she must have. She must have found somewhere to stay..." he trailed off, a flicker of pain crossing his features.

"Let's start in Fort Mindir," I said.

Jake looked up at me, nodding. "All right."

The first rays of sunlight painted the sky in hues of pink and gold as we loaded our packs onto our backs and made way to the portal room. Mae greeted us as we entered.

"Fort Mindir, please, Mae." Jake said.

When we stepped out of the portal, the air was crisp and cool, filled with the scent of dew-covered grass and the faint aroma of woodsmoke.

"Ready?" I asked.

"Yeah," Jake said, his voice gruff with emotion. "Let's do this."

We wandered through the stone streets; residents eyeing us as we passed. Fort Mindir was the next largest city in Zalindor, with a stone wall around it for sanctuary from enemies — my mother had told me. I smiled at the thought of her.

My mind drifted to Tori, to the pain and fear that must have driven her to flee. I couldn't imagine the weight of the guilt she must have felt, the terror of knowing that she had the power to hurt those she loved most, while I had the power to heal — although, not anymore. My heart dropped into the pit of my stomach.

"Maybe the inn?" Jake's voice snapped me out of my own misery.

"Yeah, let's try there."

We entered the inn, pushing open the white painted door. Despite the light colours of the building outside, the walls and furniture within were shades of browns and blacks. Half of the tables and chairs were occupied by residents, and the moment they spotted us, heads turned, eyes trailing us as we took in the bar scenery before us. *Had we walked into an inn or a bar?*

A grizzled man, with a weather-beaten face, eyed us suspiciously as we approached the bar.

"What brings you 'ere?" he asked, his eyes focused on me.

"Are you the innkeeper?" I asked.

He narrowed his eyes. "Depends who's askin'."

I leaned forward, meeting his gaze with a steady one of my own. "We're searching for someone," I said, keeping my voice low. "A friend who's gone missing. We think she might have passed through here."

The innkeeper's eyes narrowed further, and he shook his head. "Ain't seen no strangers 'round here, 'cept you."

Jake stepped forward. "Kieran is a newbie, he's no stranger."

The innkeeper hesitated, his gaze flickering between us, the wheels turning in his head, as he looked me up and down.

"No, 'aven't seen no girl," he said, picking up a glass and wiping it down with his tea towel.

"Look," Jake said, his voice low and intense. "We're just looking for someone who has really white long hair and—."

"Sorry, no outsiders 'ave been through in the past few weeks," the innkeeper said. "If yer friend doesn't want her be found, perhaps try Nirdra, or even humanville."

"Humanville?" I said, raising my eyebrows.

"Outside of Zalindor." Jake answered.

I cleared my throat. "Oh, right."

"Sorry I couldn't be of more 'elp, gentlemen," the innkeeper moved away to serve his customers.

We turned our backs, ignoring the eyes that followed us out the door of the inn.

THREE YEARS LATER

Eleven

L EANING ON THE balcony of my room, I took a deep breath as dawn broke above the scattered clouds that seemed to always hover below Myrdreya.

Three years I had been living here.

Three years since my parents' death.

Three years since Tori had left Jake.

Three long years since I started training, heightening my skills in both daggers and magic, and being a guardian for the daughter of our enemy. A daughter I had to protect, regardless of the fact, her parents' killed mine, and regardless of her having not even a scrap of magic in her veins. She was ordinary, and so boring to watch over. But, I had to be thankful. Thankful I had a home. Thankful I had friends. Thankful I had other missions to drown out my boredom.

A pounding knock on my door startled me from my thoughts. I left the balcony and crossed the room. *Were they trying to break the door down or something?* Pulling the door open, a fist froze in midair—no doubt about to break my door down if I hadn't answered.

"Finally," the man mumbled. "I've been knocking, but you weren't answering. I was told you were in your room, but I didn't fancy catching you naked."

I raised my eyebrows. "I wasn't naked. I was…on the balcony."

"Right, well, Demetri and the council would like to see you right away," the man turned away. "Best hurry."

I sighed. "Yeah, yeah…they don't like waiting…" I grumbled to myself, stepping out into the corridor and closing my bedroom door. *Do they have news on the girl?*

I picked up my pace as I crossed the floating land, almost breaking into a run on the ramp up to Demetri's tower. It wasn't often I was summoned, except for a new mission; although usually the missions came to me on a piece of paper, shoved under my door.

Strolling up the long spiralling ramp, I looked out over the city. It was magnificent; the view from his tower was the greatest view of all. When I reached the top landing, Demetri was standing outside his door, tapping his fingers on the door handle.

"Oh, about time," he huffed, his fingers curled

around the handle.

I cleared my throat, stepping up in front of Demetri. "Sorry. I came as soon as your message was delivered to me. I was on the balcony and hadn't heard the knocking."

"Right, okay, shall we?" Demetri lifted his chin, indicating with his head for me to enter.

I nodded, entering his room, and stopped short when the room wasn't empty.

All eyes on me. I swallowed.

The door closed behind me, and Demetri passed me, moving swiftly over to his desk. He didn't seat himself, though. He placed his hands on the desk. As per usual, no hair on his head was out of place—gelled I would say—perfectly into spikes. I wished I could say the same about mine, but I had a stubborn piece of hair that dangled over my forehead refusing to ever be tamed.

I gazed around the room at the other Soul Weavers within it. The tiny tower room seemed a bit cramped with this many people in it. I waited to be spoken to; the silence was deafening.

"Kieran, these are the other council members," Demetri's voice brought my attention back to him. "You may have seen them wandering Myrdreya from time to time. They live all over Zalindor, in the towns and other places. Council members are put in place to ensure the safety of Soul Weavers on Zalindor and outside of it." Demetri pushed off his desk, standing tall and boring into my eyes.

I shifted on my feet, my palms sweating. *Was I in trouble? Had I done something wrong?*

After a long moment, he smiled. "We have agreed that you have shown potential," Demetri said, his arms wide.

The council member's eyes burned holes in my skin. I swallowed, staying silent.

"Over the past few years you have shown us you can guard a girl for hours on end, which has to be the most boring mission of all, without complaint. You have shown us you value the lives around you, even saving Jake when he had been badly wounded during a mission." Demetri said.

I wiped my palms on my pants.

"Jake tells me your training has gone exceptionally well, and you are as good as he is with daggers."

The corner of my mouth quirked up. "Thank you."

"You've been learning portals over the past few months, I hear."

I nodded. "Yes. I'm getting a lot better at them."

"Excellent, good to hear."

The council members continued their silence, watching me with curious eyes.

"Kieran, we would like you to join the council."

His words rang in my ears and I blinked. *Had I heard that right?*

"We believe you may have great potential in being a leader," Demetri continued. "So, we would like you to join us. This means you'll be invited to all council meetings, you'll be informed of any new Soul Weavers that have come to light, and you'll do your duty to your people to protect them no matter the cost."

"Sir, I don't know what to say," I breathed.

"Say yes," Demetri smiled.

A wide grin spread across my face. "Yes."

Demetri stepped forward, outstretching his hand. "Welcome aboard the Council."

I took his hand, his grip was strangling around mine. "Thank you, Sir."

"Kieran, you may call me Demetri, not Sir," he said.

I nodded. "Right."

Demetri moved back behind his desk, sitting down. "We have been tracking Julianne and Jay for years, much longer than you think."

I frowned, crossing my arms over my chest.

"They abandoned Trixie when she was quite young, when they rebelled against the council. We've been searching for clues on their hideout ever since. When they attacked your parents, that was the first time we had heard news of them in years," he shifted in his seat. "Then, we finally found the whereabouts of their daughter and we were concerned they would come back for her if she showed any hints of magic, and turn her into a Dark Soul Weaver like themselves. So, we sent you to discreetly be her guardian."

I nodded, unsure why he was listing out what I obviously already knew.

"While watching over Trixie, if you find any clues of

her parents' whereabouts, or any hints that she could already be secretly working with them, please report it directly to me at once," Demetri said.

"Of course," I said, straightening my back, uncrossing my arms and letting them hang beside my body.

"Okay, dismissed for today," he waved a hand and the council members filed out.

Twelve

OVER THE FOLLOWING months, I stepped into my new position as a council member. Jake and Clara were thrilled for me—neither of them had been offered the position and both admitted they wouldn't want it even given the opportunity. Thankfully, that made it easy for us to continue being friends.

I could portal further and further around the world after months of training with the portal keeper Mae.

While my healing gift had remained dormant, I tried to keep positive, focusing my thoughts on mastering magic, portals and close combat. I had been no good with a bow, so I avoided those weapons at all costs, leaving them to Clara.

Another two years on, and I was one of the best; thanks to Jake and Clara for their excellent teaching skills.

The identity of the young girl who had taken my gift was still unknown, and the search for her had long been pushed aside. The Council's focus was on finding Julianne and Jay, and finding out what they were planning.

There had been no sight of them. No hints of them contacting their daughter either.

I had been the guardian of their daughter for over five years. She still had no idea that I sat outside in her tree for hours and hours on end, watching over her. I used to despise her. Now, I tolerate her because I didn't have a choice.

She had a boyfriend for a while, but he eventually stopped visiting, and her whole mood changed. The chirpy personality she once had disappeared and she sat staring ahead of herself for hours. I wondered if I should pity her, but then I remembered her parent's killed mine, and the fragment of pity I had disappeared.

Now, I was just plain bored of watching the most uninteresting person on the planet earth. She ate, worked and slept. Her life was snore-ville.

The shadows wrapped around me like a cloak as I walked through the dense forest toward Trixie's house, yet again. The winter air felt thick and heavy, clinging to my skin.

Clara wasn't with me this time. She had another mission—every now and then she was called away on other missions, and Demetri insisted I continued being the guardian of the girl who still hadn't showed me any sign of magic.

I sighed as I exited the cover of the trees and stared at the all too familiar house. Sighing again, I sauntered over to the window and peered in.

My eyes widened at the red-haired girl lying on the ground, her neck clearly broken. The lack of the rise and fall of her chest caused my heart to pound hard behind my ribs. I cupped my hands against the glass, and spotted the front door wide open.

Shit. Shit. FUCK.

I bolted around to the front of the house, but something caught my eye in the street. I stared ahead at a girl running down the street—bare footed—the familiar platinum blonde hair flowing down her back as she ran. She looked over her shoulder and my heart skipped a beat.

Trixie.

A bulky black-haired man bolted after her, and I didn't hesitate. My boots pounded on the tarmac as I sprinted up the road after them. Trixie dove down an alleyway and out of sight. I changed course, heading down the street parallel to the street she had just been running along. *That alleyway would surely meet up with the next street, right?*

A few houses up there was an alleyway I hoped was

the one she had bolted down. I willed my legs to move faster, pushing myself harder than ever to catch up to her before her pursuer did.

I turned down the alleyway. The man ran down from the opposite end, and Trixie staggered half way down the alleyway.

I stopped, staring at her. Her eyes widened and she, too, stopped. Her head flicked between her pursuer and me as if she was deciding who looked more menacing.

"DUCK!" I yelled, holding out my hand.

Trixie dropped to the ground without hesitation, slamming her hands into the gravel. A fireball of violet left my palm and flew down the alleyway, over Trixie, hitting the man in the chest. He fell to the ground with a thump.

I jogged toward the girl I didn't want to save. I hadn't once seen any scrap of magic come from her. Not even now. *She couldn't be that bad, could she? Maybe she didn't even know anything about magic?*

Her ice-blue eyes found mine, tears streaming down her cheeks. I placed my hands on her shoulders and carefully pulled her to her feet. She stared through her watery eyes at me, searching my face. She gazed at the lose strand hanging down my forehead, then she wiped the tears away with the back of her hand.

"Let's go," I stated, turning and starting back down the alleyway.

"But—."

I paused, turning back to her. "—No time to explain.

He will wake up in a few minutes, and we have to get you out of here."

I could see a thousand thoughts racing through her head as I watched her; impatience was gnawing at me, but I wouldn't get her to come with me if I was abrupt with her. I took a breath and relaxed.

"My name is Kieran." I held out my hand.

Trixie glanced down at my hand; the tension in her shoulders evident. Her hand stretched out, but not toward me; she placed it on her head as she looked over her shoulder at the unconscious Soul Hunter metres behind her.

She visibly shivered as a cool breeze wafted through the alleyway, and I stepped forward grasping her hand in mine. Steering her away from her pursuer, I pulled her along beside me down the street, back toward the forest.

"Hurry," I said, "we don't want him to follow."

"Who was that man and why was he—" she choked.

Okay, be nice, she just lost her friend. Say something comforting.

"I'm sorry about your friend."

She frowned as she looked up at me. "How—?"

"I will explain everything when we are in a safe place," I promised, as we reached the edge of the forest.

Her hand released from my grip and I stopped to gaze back at her.

"It's okay. Don't be afraid."

She glanced back down the street toward her house.

"I'm sorry, you can't go back home. He will expect

you to go back to your friend," I said, watching her closely. "Come, before he sees us."

She took a deep breath and headed into the trees. I turned and began running; I could hear her laboured breathing and heavy footsteps behind me. Thankfully, we weren't trying to be quiet, or we'd be screwed.

I hauled myself over fallen tree branches and roots, hurrying to get far enough into the forest before I created a portal out of here.

I slowed when we came to a tiny clearing in the trees. Out of the corner of my eye, Trixie's figure came to a halt next to a tree where she leaned on its trunk gasping for air. *Bloody amateur. Surely she's got no magic?*

I turned away from her and stared ahead. "We're here."

She remained silent, yet her breathing wasn't. I scanned the surrounding trees, listening for any movement. Nothing. *Good.*

Turning toward the large tree near the clearing, I stretched out my right hand and closed my eyes. I had created plenty of portals before, but I needed to remove her from my vision to concentrate. The daughter of my parents' murderers standing right next to me—not what I had expected today—or ever.

Okay, stop thinking about her. Concentrate. Purple lit up the back of my eyelids and I almost smiled. Opening my eyes, I stared at the portal to Myrdreya.

"What…is…that?" she asked through breaths.

"A portal," I said.

"To where?" she gasped.

"Myrdreya."

About the Author

Chantelle Lambert grew up on the Sunshine Coast, Queensland, Australia. She spent much of her childhood on the Sunshine Coast before moving to Brisbane for her high school years. When she was nineteen, she moved states to the Central Coast of New South Wales where she met her husband, Ryan Lambert.

They have a beautiful daughter together who inspired her to chase her dream as a writer.

Chantelle spent a lot of her time growing up writing short stories and going off into the imaginative world. She loves the magical fantasy world in particular. She has read so many fantasy books, which have been her inspiration over the years to keep writing and to follow her dreams.

Her passion for writing and history of anxiety and depression lead her to write this fantasy novel.

Connect with Chantelle online:

www.facebook.com/pg/chantellelambertauthor
https://www.goodreads.com/chantellelambert
www.chantellelambert.com.au

What's coming next?

Dragonshifter Redemption

What if you were cursed to transform into a dragon during the day against your will, and every month the transformation takes longer and longer to become human again?

Dragonshifters and witches are at war.

When the Dark Witch of the Nightshade Coven sacrifices Ace Stormblade's entire clan, Ace makes it his mission to get revenge and seek the cure for his curse.

He didn't expect to fall for his enemy, and be fighting along side of a witch.

Will Ace find the cure to his curse?

Or will be doom his life to become a full dragon forever, for loving the enemy?

Coming 2025

Follow for lastest updates: www.facebook.com/pg/chantellelambertauthor